CW00503482

MATING THEORY

SKYE WARREN

Two roads diverged in a yellow wood,
And sorry I could not travel both
And be one traveler, long I stood
And looked down one as far as I could
To where it bent in the undergrowth;

Then took the other, as just as fair,
And having perhaps the better claim,
Because it was grassy and wanted wear;
Though as for that the passing there
Had worn them really about the same,

And both that morning equally lay
In leaves no step had trodden black.
Oh, I kept the first for another day!
Yet knowing how way leads on to way,
I doubted if I should ever come back.

I shall be telling this with a sigh
Somewhere ages and ages hence:
Two roads diverged in a wood, and I—
I took the one less traveled by,
And that has made all the difference.

—*Robert Frost*

Prologue

Sutton

TEARING THE MOLD off bread so I have something to eat.

A black eye on the first day of school. Two dollars to my name.

Rock bottom looks different every time, but it's never looked like an empty bottle of Jim Beam until tonight. My daddy told me I wasn't better than him, and I told him to go fuck himself. He punched me in the stomach, and I told him again. And again. And again, until I spit blood onto the worn gray carpet of our single-wide.

Always had more pride than sense, which I guess is how I ended up on top of a hollowed-out building. I'm surrounded by the biggest goddamn block party without a single drop to drink. Only Harper St. Claire could have turned the razing of a prized old building into a celebration.

Half the city showed up for the big demolition. They're dancing on the bones of that long-abandoned library, praying for a fresh harvest like it's a sacrifice.

Christopher and Harper, they're the gods in this ritual.

They're the ones we pray to.

A sound makes me tense. This may be a hollowed-out fucking building, but it's *my* hollowed-out fucking building. Some of the veneer that lets me wear a suit and smile and pretend I'm in control of myself has broken down. It crumbled along with the library when the wrecking ball crashed into it. There's only the feral part of me now, and my back's against the wall. I'm ready for a fight.

The rusted metal stairs creak and whine at someone's weight.

My skin ripples with awareness. I can almost imagine the hair on my back rising up like some kind of wild animal. I'm two seconds away from baring my teeth. You don't come near someone bleeding, even if the pain is only on the inside. Really fucking poetic, watching the two people I'm in love with end up with each other. Even from ten stories high I can see the way her eyes shine when she looks at him.

And I can see the way his body tightens when

he looks at her.

A head appears over the rim of the building, blocking my view. The girl is hallowed by the spotlights on the street, her hair almost shimmering from the force of the light behind her. Or maybe it only looks that way because I'm wasted. "This roof's taken," I say, my voice hard. "Now fuck off."

She does not fuck off.

Instead I'm treated to the sight of backlit breasts and a slender silhouette as she climbs onto the roof. I made a chair out of an old radiator. Front row seats to heartbreak. Maybe she's one of Harper's friends from prep school. It might be a good time for her, watching me pant over what I can't have. She stretches her legs out in front of her, settling in beside me, using her warmth like a weapon against my numbness. "You excited about the park?" she says, her tone challenging.

"Hardly."

"It's going to revitalize the west side of Tanglewood." A spitfire, this girl. Her sarcasm so sharp I can feel it against my throat like a blade. "All the sad little poor people can finally see what a flower looks like. They'll have art and plants and magic, so who cares that they don't have food?"

Not a friend from prep school. Maybe she's

some kind of do-gooder in Tanglewood, an activist, a volunteer, working with the poor. "Why are you at the groundbreaking for a park you don't want?"

"I could ask you the same question." She holds up my bottle to the sliver of orange sunset. It gleams empty. "How long have you been up here, anyway?"

I climbed those shaky metal stairs to the roof before the first crush of steel against concrete. The crowd gasped when the dust cleared, their eyes on the two-story painting revealed on the building behind. I was too busy watching the only two people I've ever loved share a private kiss on the scaffolding that serves as their temporary stage. And then drinking, drinking, drinking. I'm not sure I could make it back down the stairs without breaking my neck, so I'm trapped here.

How long have you been up here, anyway? "It feels like a goddamn lifetime."

Her gaze follows mine. A woman throws her arms around a man's neck. He leans down to whisper in her ear. They could have been any couple in love. "Which one?" she says, her voice soft.

"Which one what?"

"Which one broke your heart?"

I couldn't describe the sledgehammer I'd taken to the brain when I met Christopher in a dimly lit private club. Too dark to be called lust or even love. Competitive and all-consuming. I couldn't describe the desire that slammed through me when I met his stepsister.

There was no way I could choose between them, but it had not been a choice. They wanted each other. Electricity crackled in the air whenever they were in the same room.

Well, I could be happy for them.

That's what a good man would do. A gentleman, and I've worked so fucking hard to pretend that's what I am. Until the liquor stripped my skin away. Until this girl sat beside me, asking which one broke my heart. She watches me with clear eyes, her gaze impossibly wise. What does she see?

"Both of them."

A sympathetic sound that feels like a stroke to my cock.

She doesn't look shocked that I fell for a man, even though it shocked the hell out of me. I questioned my sexuality, fought with it—lost myself to it. Wanting Harper did not diminish wanting Christopher.

There's something worldly in that dark gaze.

Any other day I would find out what.

Tonight, I don't care. She isn't a person with wants and dreams and needs of her own. I'm going to use her body the same way they used mine. I'm going to take what they took from me.

"Your name," I say, though it doesn't really matter.

"Ashleigh." She sounds uncertain for the first time tonight, her name drawn out into two parts. *Ash*, like the soot in a fireplace. And *leigh*, *leigh*, *leigh*. She's beautiful, and I'm wasted.

"Come here, Ashleigh." Except I don't give her a chance to come here. She might use it to leave, to disappear down that metal staircase where I can't follow.

My hand wraps behind her neck, pulling her close. My lips are harsh against hers, hungry and hard. I want to punish her for the emptiness inside me, except when she makes a little sound of fright, it fills me up with something else. Pleasure like black velvet, the kind of darkness I want to stroke my fingers over, back and forth, to feel the fibers pull against me.

Her shuddery breaths are like water, and I drink and drink. My tongue slides against hers. It's a graphic act, this kiss. More obscene than actual sex could be. More invasive as I push her head back and explore her mouth, not waiting for permission, not leaving any place untouched.

I must taste like whiskey, but she doesn't pull away.

I'm the one who breaks the kiss, panting hard. Liquid dark eyes stare up at me.

Surprise. More than that. There's outright shock in her expression. Is she younger than I thought? More innocent than anyone I ever met? I should ask her about sex, but those aren't the words that come out of my mouth. "Have you ever been in love, Ashleigh?"

A slow shake of her head. "No," she whispers.

"Good. That's good."

"I can pretend."

"What?"

"For a hundred dollars."

There's a drum in my head, pounding, pounding, telling me I've got something wrong. Really wrong. "A hundred dollars," I repeat, wishing my veins weren't running hot with liquor.

"For an hour. I know how much that suit costs. You can afford it."

I pull back, moving careful so I don't tip over. "What are you talking about?"

A cool breeze skates over us, and she shivers. I want to comfort her, but that's not what this is about. A fast fuck on an abandoned rooftop while the sounds of a massive block party bounce off the buildings around us. And a hundred dollars, apparently. Jesus. I was about to fuck a prostitute.

What's worse is that I still want to do it. More, because I know she'll let me do anything.

For a price.

I fumble for my wallet, and she tenses. Maybe it's her first time selling that sweet little body? Except that worldliness in her eyes... it's not the first time. My cock is rock hard in my slacks. I pull out the wad of cash that's inside and press it into her hand without saying a word. A few hundred, I think. "Take it."

I want to use this girl, but I'm not going to use her like this.

She scoots herself back, only an inch. There's shame on her face. And hurt, like maybe this rejection matters even though I gave her money.

"I should go," she says, not quite meeting my eyes.

"This roof's taken," I remind her, gently this time.

I don't tell her to *fuck off* again, but she gets the message. She scrambles to the edge of the roof and throws her leg over without looking back, taking the money with her. I watch the shadow of her ass in the moonlight, the same way a predator might watch its prey scamper off on a hot Sahara day. Sometimes it's too much trouble to catch something to eat, sometimes survival is more trouble than it's worth. I could have had her for a hundred dollars.

A faint scratch of metal against concrete, and then she's gone.

Back into the seething mass of partygoers, the ocean of joy that I can't join. I'm stuck on this island, and for maybe the first time, I'm glad of it. What I wanted with her wasn't good or clean. It wasn't kind.

The scaffolding where Harper and Christopher had stood is empty. The people around it still do their ritual dance, but the gods are no longer listening. Having sex, that's what the gods are doing now. I can't see them, but I know it as surely as I feel the bass reverberate through the old building holding me up. I can imagine Harper's red lips and Christopher's dark eyes. There is no girl to use. Ashleigh. Ash. Leigh. I pick up the empty bottle of Jim Beam, the proof that I'm no better than my daddy, and throw it against the ledge of the roof, watch it shatter into a million sharp glittering pieces.

Chapter One

Sutton

POUNDING WAKES ME up.

Meetings must have run late in California. I probably took the red-eye back to Tanglewood. The plane was almost empty, only a few rumpled businessmen like me and a sleepy family with Disney stuffed animals grasped in chubby hands. The airport, a ghost town. I bought a cup of lukewarm coffee on the way out so that I could make the drive home. The important thing is that I made the deal.

That's always been the important thing.

The pounding grows louder, and I groan. I'm more than tired. Hungover? Maybe I stopped by Christopher's place and had a celebratory drink. One. Maybe two.

I swallow down stale vomit. *Jesus.*

Every muscle screams a protest when I move my head. Sharp rays of light pierce my dry eyes.

The digital clock face says it's four thirty in the afternoon.

That doesn't make any sense. My alarm should have woken me up at six. I would be in the office by seven, ready to work on the next deal.

Pain lances through my stomach, making my whole body shudder.

I've never been sick a day in my life, but maybe I finally caught the flu. Or something worse. Ragged breaths saw in and out of me. I push up from the sofa, squeezing my eyes shut tight against the wild swirling of the room. What the hell's in the water in California?

"Sutton? Don't make me break down the door."

That would be Hugo, and I snarl against the memories that want to flood me. He has no business showing up here. No business making all that noise.

I stagger to the door, barely able to see, leaning against the door as it opens.

My old friend looks disgustingly un-drunk in a crisp navy shirt and well-tailored slacks. "You look like shit," he says, brushing past me into the house.

"Why are you here?"

"Your house looks like shit," he adds, taking

in the empty bottles and broken furniture. I'm not sure exactly when that happened. The realization hits me like a goddamn wrecking ball—I wasn't in California closing a business deal. I wasn't on a red-eye flight. I haven't even gone to the fucking office in weeks. I've been drunk off my ass instead of working.

I swallow the bile in my mouth. "What day is it?"

A dark glance. "You don't remember?"

"What fucking day is it?"

"I thought I'd check on you, because maybe you'd be moping. I didn't know you'd completely implode."

I've been wasted for six weeks. Six months. I push past him to the living room, shoving aside dirty clothes and a pizza box. I find my phone between the sofa cushions, the screen black. Dead.

There's a roar that must be me. Frustration. An animal kind of fury. I hurl the phone across the room. It hits the wall with an ominous *crack*. "Why shouldn't I get wasted? Everything's gone to shit."

Hugo leans against the doorframe, looking almost bored. "At this point I can't argue with you. This place is a pigsty. Where's your sister?"

"She left." That's what everyone does. They

leave.

He curses softly. "The wedding is tomorrow, you bastard."

I'd had fourteen-hour days of hard labor, my muscles burning, my stomach growling. My body was a tool, hard and sharp. I didn't worry about how the hammer felt, whether the ax needed a break. My arms carried what I told them to. My legs walked me where I needed them, except for now, when they could not help me stand. Knees folded, and I sank, graceless and heavy onto the sofa.

"Tomorrow," I say, my voice hollow.

"I suppose you could skip it."

"I haven't eaten in forty-eight hours."

"Though unless something changed, you're the best man."

The best man. As if that weren't fucking ironic, that the woman I wanted picked someone else. He was clearly the best man. She's marrying him, and I have to stand beside them and look happy.

Stale alcohol churns in my stomach. A sudden clench. And then I'm halfway across the room, stumbling over piles of mail and empty pizza boxes. The bathroom smells rank from the last time I threw up, the acidity enough to push me over the edge. It rushes out of me with a force that leaves me breathless, gasping, eyes burning. Liquid curls over the edge of the sink, splattering the mirror, the wall, me.

My fists clench the ledge, the marble I picked out. An antique repurposed frame holds a thick mirror with anti-fog features. Which means I can see my bloodshot eyes, familiar and blue and broken. The ones I saw every night before my daddy punched me in the stomach.

When I can move without heaving again, I make my way to the shower. Enough room to fit three people, but there's only me—story of my life. The polished brass knob turns in complete rotation. It takes thirty seconds for the water to be scalding, thanks to modern technology.

I pull off my clothes and step inside, forcing myself into the spray. It hits me in the face, hard enough, hot enough to make me gasp. I close my eyes. That's the only concession. The water burns me all the way to my bones. I need the pain, need to feel something, anything. It cleans me; it dissolves me into smoke and steam before turning me back into man again.

Time stopped ticking along when the two people I cared about most walked away. It could be twenty minutes I spend in the shower, feeling the water turn lukewarm. It could be two hours;

the cold turns me to marble, a statue with rivulets running down my body, steady runnels defining muscles honed from decades of labor, creating a sheen on the column of my cock.

A brushed steel drain breaks apart the stone floor, gathering water as clear as it came out of the spray. There are days' worth of dirt on me, decades' worth. I was born with too much dirt to ever wash away, but as always, it can't actually be seen; I can only feel, and God, I feel it.

Chapter Two

Ashleigh

I GET TO the old sugar factory by the time the sun breaks.

Sugar should be sweet, but everything smells burnt here. Bitter and dark. Apparently the way you made sugar was to cook it to death. The window creaks as I pull myself through the bent frame and broken boards, the glass long gone.

Opening my hands, I drop to the floor. Dust rises in a burnt cloud. I climb the wooden steps, carefully avoiding the weak spots, until I reach the top floor. Buildings crowd from every angle. Sometimes it feels like they're leaning toward me. I like to be high enough to see the sky.

This whole area used to be farmland. The sugar cane and corn were grown in fields around us, worked by prison labor after the civil war. The city ate through the agriculture land the way rust eats metal, leaving the factory an empty husk.

It's the place I call home.

Sugar's waiting for me at the top. She winds around my ankles, meowing so I know she's mad about how long I've been gone. "I haven't been on vacation," I tell her. "I've been working."

An aggrieved meow doesn't accept that excuse.

"Don't fuss. I brought you dinner." I pull a can of cat food out of my bag and turn it over on the floor in the dark spot where I usually feed her.

The irony is that she's better equipped to survive than I am. She catches rats and birds with startling regularity. They show up on my feet while I'm sleeping, which is gross and a little bit sweet. There's something very wrong when I envy a cat. Her food just wanders around, the slightest bit slower than her. She doesn't have to smile at strange men and get on her knees.

Then I fall on my worn pile of blankets. There's my small pile of treasure—books I stole from the library. Emily Dickinson and Robert Frost. A little Whitman for when I'm feeling intense. There's a small selection of clothes I've gotten from the thrift shop FREE bin.

I pull out my feast. Two-day-old hot dogs are the real prize of the day. I set one aside and eat the other in three bites. I'm slower working on a dented can of expired chili. It doesn't smell much different from Sugar's food. She licks the last bits from the floor with dainty care and then goes to work cleaning her mottled white-and-beige fur.

Creaks from the stairs make her scamper away. I straighten, holding my plastic fork like a weapon until spiky blue hair peeks over the ledge.

Ky has this lanky walk that makes him look carefree, even though I know better. He's younger than me, but he's been on the streets longer. He taught me what to charge, how to protect myself. Most of all he taught me how to please the men.

"Something smells good," he says, slinging one leg over one of the old desk chairs. It creaks beneath his weight, even though he's skinny as a string bean.

I hand over the hot dog without getting up. "Saved one for you."

He eats half in a single bite. And then the other half. His mouth is still full of dry sausage when he mumbles, "Some guys would pay money just to watch me do that."

My cheeks flame. "I didn't expect you back so soon."

"Mr. Monopoly's hostile takeover had some kind of urgent problem." Some rich guy takes Ky to his penthouse for days at a time. He's only been gone one night.

"How much did you get?"

He gives me a cheeky grin. "One thousand."

"Holy shit."

"Yeah, someone was feeling generous. He probably bought and sold Boardwalk since I saw him last." A slight frown. "He looked tired though."

My chest constricts. "Don't."

"I'm not getting attached. Don't worry. Just making sure the money train stays running. Besides, this will keep us flush in cat food for—what? Two weeks. You don't have to work."

"Don't say that."

"What? We have the money. So what's the point in being miserable."

"I'm not taking your money. I'll hold my own weight."

An eye roll. "It's not like I suffered through it. Mr. Monopoly even sucks dick. Imagine that. I seriously doubt any of the assholes who take you into the alleyway are willing to return the favor. Don't let pride keep you hungry."

Don't let pride keep you hungry. That's something he's said to me before.

Ky helped me so much. He's the one who told me to stay near the Den. Other pimps and criminals don't poach on Damon Scott's turf. And he doesn't take a cut from the whores on his street corner. That makes it a prime piece of real estate.

"I'm not going to be hungry. I'm going to *work*. Like you."

He doesn't say anything, but the doubt is clear on his handsome face. He found me huddling in basement stairs after my very first john, shaking from shock and horror and pain. I don't think I would have survived the night without him. Since then I've been unable to do it again. I really would let pride make me starve. My life isn't worth so much, after all.

Ky is only a couple years younger than me, but he's wiser by centuries. He studies me with soft brown eyes. "It's not always like that. You pick them like I taught you."

Rich. Horny. Those are the primary things he looks for. What you never want, he says, is someone who looks bored. Uninterested. That's someone who's gonna have to hurt you to get off, he says. "I'm going to. Tomorrow night, I'm going out. I already decided."

He reaches into his back pocket. A handful of hundreds lands on the blankets in front of me. "Go out. Don't go out. I don't fucking care."

I stare at the money with my stomach roiling. God, it would be so easy to let him take care of me. But I can't fool myself. He works for that money exactly as hard as I would have to. Maybe more. It's not right to let him do it for me.

Rich. Horny. Like the guy I found on the roof two weeks ago. Except he hadn't wanted me. He'd given me money. Like Ky. Pity money. I nudge the money off my blankets with my toes. If I get any closer, I'll probably snatch it up. "Tomorrow."

CHAPTER THREE

SUTTON

THE DEN IS a gentleman's club, which doesn't mean there are strippers. Backroom deals and plenty of alcohol. A high-end bar for the elite of the city.

At least, there aren't *usually* strippers.

I'm not sure what Hugo has in store for this bachelor party. I should have been the one planning it, but he's my friend, and he knew that I couldn't manage it myself. Well, I definitely couldn't have hosted a goddamn party. I'm not even positive I'll be able to attend it.

"Coward," I mutter when I'm still standing on the pavement.

I should be inside the building, happy that two people I love have found their happy ending. I'm not jealous. That would be too easy. I'm despairing. I'm lonely. I'm goddamn afraid that I'm always going to be this way. There's something inside me that doesn't know how to love, not truly, not deep. And Christopher? Harper? They could tell that about me.

I find Hugo inside the Den.

"Now what do you have planned for this shindig? So that I can pretend I give a damn, that is. Pin the tail on the donkey? A pinata?"

"A pinata? No. I didn't think your heart could take much more of a beating."

I study my empty glass, brooding. "Strippers?"

"That would have been too easy. Christopher said no to strippers."

My eyes narrow. "You talked to him."

"Someone had to."

The accusation doesn't have any heat behind it, because Hugo knows how much this cost me. Christopher showed up at the ranch, wearing his suit, authentically Italian, his loafers shiny against the dusty brown backdrop of my land. *I want you to be my best man,* he said, and God, fuck, no, never, I can't, it will break me, I'm already broken.

It would be an honor. That's what I said instead.

A very European one-shoulder shrug. "He understood why I contacted him, but he was very firm on the matter. No strippers. Besides, he does not seem like the type."

"The type of man who likes tits and ass, you mean?"

"The type of man who likes to pay for them."

I'm not sure how you tell them apart, but if anyone knows, it's Hugo.

There are only so many ways a man without a dollar to his name can turn pure ambition into a fortune. As a blue-eyed roughneck, construction workers welcomed me into their fold. They were all too happy to send me in to speak to the foreman, to the project manager, to the investors, when the schedule had to be delayed—and the schedule *always* had to be delayed. They sent me because they knew I would have him sign on the dotted line, with a smile on his face while he did it.

Hugo had a slightly different path.

He worked as a male escort to wealthy women who wanted an orgasm once in a while. It's not like their rich husbands were doing the job in between screwing the nanny at home and the secretary at work.

"An ice bar," Hugo says, inclining his head. "The bar made from ice, the bottles. The cups. The whole thing. It's already set up in the back room. We'll have to wear parkas."

"That must have cost a pretty penny."

"I used your credit card. You don't mind, do you?"

That earns him a wry look. "Anything for the happy couple. What about the Ferrari out front?"

"Not street legal, but we have some off-duty cops keeping a route empty through downtown."

"Are you also using my credit card to pay them off?"

"Cash only. There can't be a paper trail."

I have a hazy memory of handing over my last hundred-dollar bill to the guy delivering my pizza. *Don't fall in love,* I told him. *That's what I'm telling you. Don't you dare.*

Nothing like advice from a drunk.

The party has already hit a feverish pitch. Alcohol flows in amber pours and crystal glasses. In the center of the room Christopher stands in a crowd of men, all of them vying for his opinion, his attention. He's a goddamn prince of the business world, and the funny thing is, he doesn't particularly enjoy it. The numbers, that's what he likes. Making them add up the way he wants. This part, the people part, this was my job. Even from twenty feet away I can tell he's uncomfortable.

This is the part where I save him. Always, I

saved him.

When we were friends.

Before we became, so briefly, lovers.

In that hairsbreadth of time when there were three of us. Instead of two.

His eyes meet mine, and relief flashes through him. An instant of relief too soon replaced by wariness. Well, that's about what I deserve. I head toward him in slow, direct strides. Men and women move aside for me, curious about whether I'm going to congratulate my best friend. Or throw a punch. Tell the truth, I wasn't sure which one it would be when I showed up.

Christopher doesn't take a step back. Maybe he's willing to take that punch.

Or maybe he knows me better than I do.

I put out my hand. "Congrats," I tell him, my manner easy. "The best man won."

A rumble of laughter. Everyone around us knows we fought over the woman he's going to marry. What they don't know is that we held her sweet body between our own, making her come with our fingers and tongues. They don't know that I loved Christopher before I loved Harper.

He clasps my hand back, and he pulls in for a brief, impersonal bro hug. The warmth of his hand doesn't make my stomach flip. Maybe the alcohol has made me permanently numb. "Nah," he says, his tone as casual as mine. "I've never been the better man."

The words are simple, meaningless. Empty, if you didn't know there was an apology inside them, wrapped up so tight it can barely breathe—but there it is, from a man who never explains himself to anyone. People wander away, and then it's the two of us.

"You came," he says.

This close I can see the fine lines fanning from Christopher's eyes, early for a man so young. He'll look distinguished before he turns thirty. That comes from working late hours, always with something to prove. "Of course I came."

"Of course? I figured Hugo would have to drag you here."

Which is exactly what happened. "I wouldn't miss it for the world."

That earns me a snort. "You don't have to stay long. I'd leave early if I could."

My mind flashes on a girl with honey-brown hair and endless Bambi eyes. I do want to leave early, but it's not to go home. Not to drown myself in a bottle. I want to leave early and find her. "Is Harper having a bachelorette party?"

"Don't worry. I made her promise not to

paint tonight."

Harper St. Claire has a penchant for using art as a medium for protest and society change. Which means there's a decent chance she could end up arrested the night before her wedding. "Maybe she's somewhere making a statement about the shackles of marriage, painting a life-sized Mary Tyler Moore across your brand-new building."

"Don't give her ideas," he says darkly.

A rueful smile. "That's about all I can do now."

We stare at each other, marking the moment in time, from one second to two, passing over the space where we were best friends. It won't ever be the same. Harper changed that. Even knowing that, I can't resent her. Want her, love her. Go mad with goddamn jealousy. I can't wish that she never showed up though. It would be as insincere as wishing away the sun.

"You nervous?" I hope not. It would be a hell of a conversation if I have to convince him to man up. Still, most grooms experience jitters, don't they?

"No." The word is soft and sure.

"You always did know what you wanted." There. I don't even sound bitter about it.

"When it came to business, yes. When it came to Harper, I spent a long time in denial." He cuts himself off with a quiet curse. "I know I have to apologize."

My eyebrows rise. "For winning her?"

"God, no. I won her fair and square. I won't apologize for that." It's so Christopher that I can't help but smile. That's what I love about him. *Love.* My smile fades. He meets my gaze. "I'm sorry for not seeing what you felt... about me. I was—*am*—your friend. I should have known."

"I didn't want you to know."

A wry twist of his lips. "I didn't even know you were—"

"Bi?"

"That."

I got my ass kicked by my dad until I was old enough to punch back. I got my ass kicked at school for being my father's son, before I learned to throw a right hook so hard the person had to go to the hospital. When I realized I was turned on by both men and women, it wasn't something I was going to share with the world. "It's not something I talk about much."

A glint of amusement. "No. Hell, I would have been afraid to tell you if I were gay. You always seemed like such a Southern boy. Hunting and fishing and fighting."

"I'm a pacifist mostly. Except I do like fishing. The fish have it coming."

He looks away, toward the throngs of men who fill the space, the drinking and the gambling. The pretense that we aren't being watched. "Who the hell are all these people?"

"Friends. They're friends, Christopher."

"No. They're business. Whether we worked with them in the past or they're hoping we work with them in the future, they're here to make a buck. You were my friend. Maybe the only one."

"I'm still your friend."

"Are you?"

Unfortunately. Unfortunately, I'll always be his friend. Unfortunately, there are knives carving the inside of me, writing patterns of loss on the slick side of my skin. "Yes."

A roar goes up through the crowd, and I turn my head to see a group of women. They're wearing colorful, sequined dresses—a night on the town. Harper's in the lead, wearing a white sheath dress and a tiara that probably has real diamonds. She's also holding a giant inflatable penis, which she's augmented with a Sharpie, drawing a smiley face on the plastic and the outline of a tuxedo.

The bachelorette party has descended on the

Den.

The men are more than happy to welcome the girls, ordering rounds of shots and breathing in their lush, sweaty scents. Christopher only has eyes for his bride. His dark blue eyes deepen as she approaches. He grasps her waist and pulls her the rest of the way. Their kiss is so intimate, so raw, so *loving*, I have to look away. When Harper pulls back, her eyes are dazed.

She sees me, and she grows wary. "Hey, Sutton."

"Hey." And the Oscar goes to… Sutton Mayfair, who sounds like a human being instead of a seething mass of envy and stupid self-pity. "Having a good time?"

A relieved smile. I've fooled her. *Human,* she thinks. "The best time."

"I like your friend."

She gives the giant inflatable penis a squeezing hug, making its Sharpie-drawn eyes bulge. "Dick is our chaperone. It's not safe for young women to be on the streets alone, you know."

This is Harper—effervescent and irreverent. Being around her, you can't help but feel lighter. Christopher is the very opposite. He makes everything more serious. More weighty. They're perfect for each other, and I… well, I don't belong here.

The silence underlines that fact.

I see her ask him without words: did you ask him yet? I see Christopher answering without words: no. I've watched him do a hundred negotiations. So I know the precise moment he decides this is the time. There's cunning in the air, like electricity before a storm.

"Do you want to come over?" he asks. After. Oh God. A threesome.

That's what he's offering right now. Like I'm a gift he's giving her. *Here's your last chance to fuck someone else before we get hitched.*

Or worse, it might continue after they say *I do*. I'd be like a living, breathing vibrator in their marriage bed. The sick part is how badly I want to say yes.

I can almost taste her salt sweet skin. I can almost feel the bristle on his jaw. My body's taut with hunger. *Yes, I'll come over. Yes, I'll eat her out and suck your dick and do whatever you want. I'll leave whenever you want.*

Bile burns my throat. "No, thanks," I say, the words stiff and staccato.

"Oh." Disappointment in her eyes almost changes my mind.

I don't have to say anything else. I don't owe

them any explanation. Certainly I don't owe them any lies, but I find myself speaking anyway. "I'm seeing someone."

Christopher's blue eyes lighten. "That's great."

That probably means he's still worried about Harper changing her mind. I could reassure him that won't happen, but then he says, "You should bring her to the wedding."

"Or him," Harper says, sounding hopeful.

"Right. Maybe." No one's coming to the wedding, man or woman. I'm not seeing anyone. My facade has cracked. I can no longer pretend I'm fine. I turn toward the door and walk away, leaving the party and the two people I love behind me.

Chapter Four

Ashleigh

Cold. Hungry. There's no other word for it. *Desperate*. Everything about this life hurts, but there's nothing I would have done differently.

Sometimes life doesn't give any good choices.

Male laughter punches the silence as the door opens and closes, more men arriving. Droplets quiver on the windows. It's shaping up to be an epic party. In a few hours there'll be drunk men willing to pay two hundred dollars for me to follow them to a motel room.

As long as I don't lose my nerve, I don't have to starve tonight.

A dark sedan slows on the street. The window slides down. A man in his late forties looks me up and down. I could have passed him in a grocery store or a gas station without looking twice. An ordinary man. Gold glints from his ring finger. Of course he's married. His wife is probably at home, warm and fed, scrolling through Pinterest right now. "How much?" he asks.

Tell him two hundred dollars. Ky told me that the first time I worked this street corner. He also gave me a pack of condoms. "You let your mind go somewhere else. Do what they say, don't ask questions, and you survive. That's the important thing."

An unexpected guardian angel, for sure.

Tell him twenty dollars. Then maybe he won't expect so much. I don't know what the hell I'm doing, and I want it to be over soon. Twenty dollars is enough to buy hot French fries, salty on my tongue, and a cool, bubbly soda to wash them down. I'm almost sick with hunger.

Tell him a thousand dollars. Anything to make him drive away.

"I'm not for sale," I say, my voice catching.

"What? Speak up."

"I'm done for the night," I say, more clearly.

Anger flashes through his eyes, mixed with disdain, and I'm glad I didn't get into his car. I'm glad I didn't let him put his hands on me. It might have cost more than my dignity. "Your loss," he says, before driving away, leaving a spray of gravel on my bare legs.

Red taillights disappear behind a building,

and then I'm alone again.

Hungry and cold and desperate again.

Why couldn't I have gone with him? Spread your legs. Open your mouth. Survive. That's what Ky told me to do. It makes so much sense, but I'm stubborn. And stupid, maybe. Filled with this pointless hope that something will save me.

This isn't a fairy tale.

The door slams open, and someone steps out of the Den. He's framed by the garish, glittering light—only shadow and movement. Broad shoulders and long legs. I take a step backward without thinking about it. I've learned to trust my instincts in the past six months. Something about this man says *dangerous.*

He takes two steps forward, stopping right on the edge of the curb, his body a hard line against the whistling wind. The streetlamp limns a face with harsh grooves. Blond hair in wild disarray, curling at the ends, turning damp in the night. A trench coat and black shoes that gleam. He reminds me vaguely of a pirate. He could be standing at the bow of his ship, watching the skyline for secrets of a storm.

He turns, sudden and sharp, as if he heard me. I didn't make a sound. It's only my heartbeat that could have given me away, rapid as a rabbit.

Blue eyes narrow. "Ashleigh."

It would be better if he didn't remember my name. Better if he could have looked at my legs and my breasts the way the man in the car had done. It would be better to believe that every man would treat me like trash. Knowing that some men are good and kind and caring—but not for me, never for me—hurts worse than anything. "I'm not for sale." The words slip out before I can stop them. He didn't even ask my price.

He raises one eyebrow. "Then you'd be the only one."

Jaded. Maybe I'm not the only one determined to think the worst of the world. "Is that how you think of women? They aren't all out to get your money."

For a moment I think he's going to stride away. He'll disappear into the night. Hours from now I'll be wondering if he were real. The possibility hangs in the night like dew. It's what he wants to do. What he *should* do. Everything about him, from his clothes to his manner, speaks of a man with manners. With a real job and a real house and a real girlfriend. He shouldn't be talking to me.

Then he turns toward me, decisive. In a moment he's in front of me. Another second, and

I'm backed up against the stone bricks of the Den. "It's not how I think of women, sweet thing. It's how I think of everyone. Men included."

"Do you have a price?" I manage to ask, even though it's risky to talk back to a man. Especially when his large frame has me tacked to the wall like a freaking butterfly. This close I can see the shadow of hair on his jaw, the mole beside his right eye.

"Yes. Me." A harsh laugh. "I've got a price. It's not even a high one."

"What is it?" It's like a street urchin wandering into Tiffany's, this question. It doesn't matter what the answer is. The number will always be too high. Whether he wants a society wife or a mother for his children, it will never be me.

"A kiss."

The word lodges in my skin, sharp and hot. "A kiss?"

There's challenge in those blue eyes. And pitiless knowledge. "A kiss is all it takes for me to fall head over heels. I'd believe I was in love with you, build a fucking castle in the sky, because I'm that kind of idiot, aren't I?"

A whisper. "Two hundred dollars."

His gaze drops to my lips. "I thought you weren't for sale."

I changed my mind when he talked about castles in the sky. He's still in love with someone else. That much is clear from the bitterness in his voice. I can't be that woman, but I can pretend for a single night. Somewhere warm. His arms.

"Two hundred dollars and your name."

That earns me a clap of laughter. "My name."

"And dinner." I don't know where I get the courage. Dinner means I don't need to eat for another two days. Two hundred dollars means I'm set for another two months.

His name should mean nothing to me.

He bows his head, hiding his eyes. A droplet of rain falls from his hair to my chest. "Christ. What the hell happened to you? No, don't tell me. I can't listen to a sob story and still fuck you, and I really want to fuck you."

Sob story. That about sums it up. There's a hole in my chest where those words hit me. Seared edges from the realization that I'm that transparent. That every man who's wanted to fuck me, who's offered me money, the man who rolled down his window, they *knew*. Maybe not the specifics, but they knew enough. Women don't stand on street corners because things were going okay.

"Fuck." He reaches into his coat pocket.

Something slim and black. He opens it and finds money. Hundred-dollar bills, I realize, as he shoves them into my hand. Two of them. "Take it. And get the fuck off the street before someone like me drags you home and makes you cry."

The money is still warm from the heat of his body. I clench the bills in my fist. Emotion chokes my throat. *Thank you.* I can't make myself say the words.

He turns away, not waiting for gratitude, ready to disappear into the night.

"A kiss," I manage to say, and he stops.

CHAPTER FIVE

SUTTON

I'M TURNED AWAY from the Den, my hands into my pockets, head down. The night is caught somewhere between rain and clear. Beads of moisture gather on the sleek black fabric of my suit. Fog mutes the sound of my dress shoes on pavement.

The entire world narrows to the woman behind me. *A kiss.*

Leave. Walk away. Don't fuck a girl that broken.

I know about the underbelly of Tanglewood. And I know better than to think I can solve problems that thick. A few Benjamins aren't going to change her life. But there's a difference between not helping her and actively using her. Touching her, even the lightest brush of my fingertip across her cheek, would cross a line.

She doesn't want to be here. There are women

who choose sex work without a dark history but none of them do it this way. Only the most crude and dangerous men would shop for a woman here. Men like me, apparently.

The brick wall holds her up. She looks fragile against the city. Small and fundamentally breakable. How am I supposed to leave her here? But how can I take her with me? There's only the thinnest thread between the beast inside me and the man I pretend to be. My true self, the bastard who loses everyone he loves, has never been this close to the surface.

She looks at me with unfathomable dark eyes. There's pain hidden in the depths, but I don't see that right now. I'm only looking at trust. Undeserved trust.

The corner of her lips hitches up in a private smile.

It seals her fate.

I back her up against the wall, crowding her, stealing her air.

Her eyes go wide like a doe caught in the headlights. That's me—a fucking truck. I'm going to break her to pieces. I'll break myself, too. I lean down to breathe her in. I'm not even touching her yet. I don't have my hands on that pale skin or my cock in that sweet cunt. No, I'm scenting her now. It's a fully primal move. Every veneer of civility has been stripped away. This suit is a goddamn lie. I'm an animal, getting ready to mount her, getting ready to mate.

A kiss, she said, not knowing what she tempted.

My lips brush her forehead. It should be ridiculous with my cock like iron in my slacks, but it doesn't feel ridiculous. Tenderness moves inside me, sharp enough to make me grunt. I drop my lips to the bridge of her nose. Even this much is wrong. Wrong when the woman doesn't really desire me. Wrong when she wouldn't be wet if I shoved two fingers in her pussy. I've never had a woman who was anything less than enthusiastic, but I want her too much to walk away. She stands very still as I reach her mouth. That full, pretty mouth with the garish red lipstick. I nibble away the waxy layer, searching for the dry, chapped, realness of her.

When I pull back her eyes are wide. Her nostrils flare where she breathes hard. I haven't even gotten started yet, and she already looks ready to bolt. "What was that?" she asks, her voice shaky. I want to pull her hair and spank her pretty little ass. I want to spread her legs and ride her until she sobs her climax into the sheets. And she looks shocked by a single kiss.

Anger swells inside me, inky black. "You ever have a boyfriend, Ashleigh?"

"Yes," she says, but it's so clearly a lie it makes me want to laugh. Or cry. "I know how to kiss. I know how to—how to *fuck*. But that wasn't a kiss."

The word *fuck* sounds completely foreign on her lips. It sounds like a made-up word. A Dr. Seussian exaggeration. "That was the way you kiss someone you care about."

Defiance in those brown sugar eyes. "You don't care about me."

"No," I say, even though I'm the one lying now. I'm the one exaggerating to prove a goddamn point. "I don't give a shit about you, but I never learned to kiss any other way."

That small point of a chin rises. She may not have a lick of self-preservation, but she has pride. And God, that makes me want her more. "Then maybe I can teach you something."

Grim amusement curls my lips. "You just might."

I came outside because I needed some air that hasn't been breathed in and exhaled by Harper and Christopher. I wanted to smell dirt and grass and the weather foretold on the wind. Nothing in the city can come close. Except for her. I breathe her in, and the same sense of rightness, of coming home fills me. She's like the goddamn earth— sweet and elemental.

It's almost like I conjured her up. Or maybe I'm hallucinating. Alcohol can do that to you, even if it's been eight hours since I touched a drop. If she isn't real, there's no reason not to touch her, not to fuck her. No pesky morality to keep me from paying for the privilege.

Besides, he does not seem like the type.

The type of man who likes tits and ass, you mean?

The type of man who likes to pay for them.

I've never paid for a fuck, either. It would be a new low for me. I'm full of those lately.

I bend down to nuzzle her cheek, the under-side of her jaw. Her neck. I kiss her there, and she shivers. We're standing in a cold drizzle, but she actually shivers at the feel of my lips. Ashleigh is an orchid in a snowstorm. She'll never survive.

"Come home with me," I murmur, finding the hollow at the base of her neck. Slipping my tongue out for a taste. Rainwater. The weather has slicked away her flavor.

"There's a motel," she says, breathing hard even though I have her trapped, *because* I have her trapped. "Two blocks away. The Rose and Crown. We can get a room there."

A motel that rents by the hour. "I want the whole night."

Her gaze doesn't leave mine as she shakes her head. It's a refusal that has nothing to do with money. Everything to do with her fear over a soft kiss.

I bend my head to take her mouth, searching the depths through the rain and the air until I find the elusive flavor of her, the fire of her. I drink it down and relish the burn. My palm cups her cheek, and she jumps. Only by slow degrees does she melt into my hold.

"Sutton," I say, my voice thick. "That's my name. Sutton Mayfair. Say it."

"Sutton," she whispers, and the sound makes me tighten.

Her body becomes pliant against the brick and my body. I lap at her, slow and hungry, showing her the way I'd fuck her. Not so different from the way I kiss. She may teach me how to do it rough and meaningless. That's a lesson I need to learn, but I'm going to show her how good it can be. My tongue moves against hers in a sensual glide—patient, patient, patient until she flicks her tongue in timid answer. The feel of her, the warmth, makes me ache. My cock throbs in my dress pants, and I press forward, seeking more pressure. She's boneless against me, willing—and if I could bet my entire construction business— between her legs, she would be wet.

Finally I lift my head and look into her lust-drowsed eyes. Triumph beats in my chest, as if I've proved some kind of point. Her lips are swollen and stung from my incipient beard. She waits, lax, for whatever happens next. I could kiss her sweet little cunt up against this wall, gravel digging into my knees, the wind whipping at her hair, and she'd let me.

Because you're fucking paying her.

"Two hundred dollars," I say, and she flinches, coming awake.

"That's what you gave me."

"We're not done yet."

"A kiss. That's what I offered you. That's what you took."

"And dinner," I remind her. My stomach growls as if remembering that I'm starving. Alcohol is rich in calories. It keeps me from getting hungry. "That was part of the deal. I'm going to get you dinner. What do you like? Chinese? Steak?"

She licks her lips, and I know that I have her.

It feels a little dirty, that I'd tempt her this way, this little slip of a woman, so slender I know she's gone hungry. Well, I have some experience with the feeling. The gnawing inside your stomach, as if it's going to eat you from the inside. The yawning pain that keeps you from sleeping no matter how tired you are.

I glance up the street, where you can see the bright lights of a Thai restaurant. "Curry? That's the good thing about Tanglewood. You can find every kind of food here."

"Not curry," she says, her voice trembling.

How long has it been since she ate anything? "No curry, then. You let me decide. There's a great place only a five-minute walk. You usually need reservations, but I know the owner."

CHAPTER SIX

ASHLEIGH

IF I HAD thought about dinner, I would have thought about burgers or burritos from a fast food joint. Maybe, if we were dreaming big, I would have thought about a Styrofoam container of cheese fries from the diner. I could not have imagined this place.

Intricate stained glass windows send shards of colors across pristine white tablecloths. Wooden arches soar above our heads. It was a church, the maître d' explains as he leads us to a secluded table for two. A church from the 1920s that was restored for this restaurant. The other patrons are wearing suits and evening wear. I'm in a top I found in the trash and a skirt I found in the thrift store. Did Sutton bring me here as a joke?

I glance at him, and he's watching me with challenge in his blue eyes. He expects me to balk at the fanciness, and maybe I should. I'm probably going to make a fool of myself. I have to weigh my pride against my hunger. Hunger wins.

I'm handed a large, leather-bound menu that has words I've never heard before and no prices. A bread basket arrives laden with thinly sliced raisin bread and thick slabs topped with caramelized onions. I take a piece of the onion bread with shaking hands and tear it apart. God, it's so soft. And still warm from the oven. My mouth feels like it's too full of saliva. I understand those cartoons with drooling animals in a real way. I'm not drooling, but this is how it would happen. Days without eating and then a gourmet bread basket in front of me.

I shove it in my mouth. My eyes close in unwilling ecstasy.

Sutton's lids have fallen low, and I realize I made a sound. A moan.

"I'm sorry," I whisper, already pushing more bread into my mouth. Humiliating. That's what this is. Maybe that's how he meant it. It would have been less embarrassing for him to fuck me in the street, but I can't stop eating now that food's in my reach.

"Slow down," he murmurs. "You'll give yourself a stomach ache."

How does he know? How does he know how

starving I am? I inhale two more pieces of bread before I can bring myself to speak. "You're making a joke out of me."

"No one's laughing," he says, and I have to admit that it's the truth. His blue eyes are wholly serious. And knowing. As if he understands this level of hunger.

"Then why did you bring me here? I don't belong with these people."

"These people are nothing special. The fact that they have money and you don't is mostly a matter of luck. Randomness. A game of chance, and you're losing."

I take another piece of bread and force myself to eat it in slow, steady bites. "Is that why you have money? Because you won the game?"

A ghost of a smile. "You could say that."

"Can you teach me how to play?" The question comes out before I can stop it, earnest and hopelessly naive. This is the part where Ky would shake his head. He knows about the world. About men. I'm the one stuck with my head in a poetry book.

He's saved from answering when the waiter arrives. Sutton orders a medium rare rib eye for the both of us, along with flame-grilled artichokes and beet and goat cheese salads.

The waiter leaves, and we sit in silence. The quiet clink of silver against expensive china provides a backdrop. Somewhere in this restored church, around some corner or up those stairs, someone's playing a harp.

"You want to play the game," he says, leaning back in his chair. "This is how you do it. You demand to be taken to places like this. There's always going to be some sad fucker like me willing to do it. You don't ask for two hundred dollars. You ask for a car. A condo."

He might as well be speaking another language. I understand organic chemistry better than this. "And you think men are going to pay for that?"

"They already do. They're paying some woman. Why not you?"

I look down at myself, at this body that's supposedly worth so much. It doesn't make a difference. I hardly recognize myself. My arms, my legs. My breasts. I could be walking around in someone else's skin. "That's not how you made your money."

"The world isn't fair, darling. I figure you already know that."

"I know that," I whisper, thinking about throwing a softball and father-daughter dances.

That wasn't my childhood. I got indifferent words and wandering hands. I took it and took, until one day I decided I'd had enough. I ran away from home and never looked back. No matter how cold or hungry or desperate I get on the street, I never wish I was home.

"Now I'm going to ask you again: Come home with me."

HIS HOUSE IS a ranch in the outskirts of Tanglewood. Every mile away from the west side erodes my confidence. Ky's going to freak when he gets back. I can't turn back now. Not only because I wouldn't have a ride. I can't turn back because this man wants me. For some reason, he wants me. And I need the money enough to see it through.

Headlights flash across a copse of trees. Gravel rumbles beneath the tires. He stops the car, and we sit in the quiet, with only the pops of the engine and the croak of crickets to guide us. "Having second thoughts?" he asks, his voice husky.

Yes. I'm afraid. Hold my hand. "Of course not. We made a deal."

Soft laughter. "We did."

I unlatch the seat belt and turn to face him. He looks miles away from that man earlier tonight, except I'm in the same position. Aren't I? About to have sex with a stranger. I reach over to place my palm on his thigh. It's not quite where he would want it, but it's as close as I can bring myself right now. I squeeze gently, feeling muscle and heat. It's awkward in a car. That's what I learn in the next few minutes while I propel myself closer to him, while I press a clumsy kiss to his lips. He remains seated, hands dropped to his sides, head resting back. He doesn't make any move to hold me, touch me. Fuck me. But he doesn't push me away either. And when I manage to lick across his bottom lip, he sucks in a breath.

It would be so easy for him to reach for me, for him to turn a few degrees in my direction. Then I could pretend that we were two people making out. We had gone to the college football game. He bought me a large Coke and a pretzel as big as my face. I hung on his arm while he cheered on his team. After the game he brought me home and turned to kiss me good night. One kiss turned into another. We'd both be panting, urgent. The windows would turn foggy. That's what I could pretend. Instead Sutton stays straight in his chair, watching me from beneath slitted eyes. He lets me fumble with the fabric of his slacks. At least he's hard beneath them. Very hard. Very large. Enough to make me wince in anticipated pain. There's no steam on the windows, because he isn't breathing hard. He's watching me make a fool of myself, stroking clumsily through the wool, trying to figure out how to please him. And failing.

"Do you make guys come like that?" he asks, all droll politeness.

"Yes," I snap, even though it's a lie. I pull my hand back, because clearly I was doing it all wrong. Despite his hard cock, I was doing it wrong. My words come out stiff. "If you want something different, you only have to ask."

"I didn't say I didn't like it." Shadows hold him in a tight embrace. I see glittering eyes and full lips. A square chin with gold-dark scruff. "There's something sweet about it. As if you never touched a cock before. But that can't be true, can it?"

My cheeks heat, and I'm grateful for the darkness. "Of course not."

"You make me feel like I'm in high school again."

"Is that a bad thing?"

His thumb lifts my chin. "Tell me you aren't

55

in high school."

"I'm not in high school," I recite.

"Seriously, Ashleigh. I'm going to lose my shit."

"I'm not. Really. God." Of course I'm not in high school because I dropped out six months ago. Hard to go to school when you don't have a place to sleep. Or running water. I don't bother telling him that. Let him think I'm a couple years older if it helps him sleep at night. It doesn't matter whether I'm seventeen or twenty-seven when the lights are off.

Some men are gentle. Some are rough. All of them want the same thing—my mouth wrapped around their dick. Sutton? I don't think he's different. Not when he stiffens. A groan fills the warm vehicle. My mind's already going to that faraway place where nothing and no one can touch me. I reach for the hard, throbbing heft of him in his slacks, and he grunts. "What the fuck, Ashleigh?"

I don't bother stopping, because he can catch up. He must know what I'm going to do. *A kiss.* No one pays two hundred dollars so they can lick my lips. He wants this kind of kiss. I feel his desire hot and thick in the air. My fingers find his zipper and tug, tug, tug.

He grasps my wrist, forcing me to stop. "I said, what the fuck?"

My gaze meets his. "I'm doing what you want."

"A blowjob in my driveway? No, sweet thing. Not even close."

He doesn't want a blowjob? Well, he's the first one. Panic beats against my rib cage. He'll want something I don't know how to give. Empty, brainless sex. That's what I've been taught. He wants that strange kissing and feeling and aching deep in my core.

Home was a beige house in suburbia. Ours had white crown molding and granite countertops. Those are the things that made it a nice house. An expensive house. Those things are nothing like this. Columns of stone and wood stand like sentries around the front door. Windows with little hand-welded arches march across the entrance hall. Thick plants of wood are knotted and gouged and scraped in an agreeable texture. This is not a nice house. It's a ranch-style mansion, every piece strong and rough and beautiful. Like the man who closes the door behind us. A wide-open floor plan reveals multiple seating areas, a ten-foot dining table, a kitchen with bright red appliances. My attention is drawn by a bank of tall, wide windows at the back of the house. A view of rolling hills in the moonlight takes my breath away. And is that—

"Do you have horses?"

Chapter Seven

Sutton

K NOTTED WOOD AND worn-smooth leather. This place is my sanctuary.

The shiny fake satin of her mini skirt looks out of place. Her heels wobble in the thick pile of the carpet. Part of me expects her to sit on the couch, as if I'm going to interview her before fucking her silly. Or maybe she'll drape herself across the kitchen countertops—a sexual offering. She does neither. Instead she crosses to the metal sculpture mounted across the back wall. A wild horse gallops, its hooves flying, its mane proud in the wind. She runs her hand along the curve of its breast. "It's beautiful."

Christ. Horses. With her lithe body and world-weary eyes, she looks all grown up. Then she gets excited about horses, and she could be twelve years old again. It's a strange dichotomy, one I shouldn't find alluring. Even as my brain works out the ethical implications, my blood beats with a low, primal beat. Mine. She's mine. And nothing, not even my own personal morality, will keep her from me.

"Where did you get this?"

I don't have to answer. An art gallery. Walmart. It doesn't matter where I got it. She's a prostitute. Get on your knees. That's what I should tell her. "I made it."

Her eyes widen. "You did?"

"It's nothing. A blowtorch and some scrap metal."

"What are you talking about? It's beautiful. I can feel the wind." She traces the curve of his breast with her fingertip. I can almost feel the caress across my pecs.

Her hand keeps moving, onto the mane.

"They look like flames," she says.

"Some say the world will end in fire." It's a foolish, maudlin thing to say, made even more ridiculous by the fact that she won't understand. She'll think I'm a crazy prepper or something, counting down until doomsday.

She glances back at me without missing a beat. "Some say in ice."

Surprise roots me to the ground. "From what I've tasted of desire, I hold with those who favor fire."

"But if it had to perish twice," she says, reciting the poem in a melodic voice. It's a siren song. "I think I know enough of hate, to say that for destruction ice, is also great, and would suffice."

"You like Robert Frost."

"I like poetry." She touches the tip of the mane.

I open my mouth, because the edges are rough there. They're not polished smooth, not made to be touched. Her breath sucks in. It's a quiet sound, but I feel it in my bones, that prick of pain. She pulls her hand back. I'm across the room in a few seconds, turning her palm in mine. A small drop of blood forms on her forefinger.

"Hell."

"It doesn't hurt," she whispers.

I should run her hand under water. Probably get Neosporin and a Band-Aid. And then drive her back to the street corner, because what the fuck am I doing here? Instead I dip my head and suck her finger into my mouth, licking away the salt-metal drop. Her eyes are dark pools that reflect the metal horse. When I let go of her, I expect her to back away. To cower in the corner, like I'm some kind of vampire. That's what I am, in a way. Drinking down her youth and life force.

She drops to her knees, slow and graceful, keeping her gaze on mine.

This isn't the place for it. I should take her into the bedroom, at least. Dark windows watch from every angle, miles of ranchland a witness to what I'm about to do. My cock feels hard as iron in my slacks. She's probably not even wet beneath that cheap black fabric. I want her too bad to care. I could reach down and finger her until she came, slick and swollen. I could whisper a few dirty words to make her damp.

Instead I put my hand on her head, stroking gently, feeling the shape of her, the impenetrable strength of her. I sift her hair through my hands. It's a pale straw color, but it doesn't feel like straw. It feels soft and pliant. Like her.

"You gonna take me in your mouth, sweet thing?" My accent comes out thicker when I'm aroused. It's thick as goddamn molasses right now.

She nods slowly. "If that's what you like."

"There's no man alive who wouldn't want that pretty mouth."

A blush darkens her cheeks. "Should I—?"

She doesn't finish the question. Her hands go to my belt. She fumbles with the hammered gold clasp and the soft leather. Next she works on the button. The zipper, which curves over the bulge of my erection. She goes slower there, as if careful she might hurt me. I'm hard enough to pound steel. Her gentle hands won't do a bit of harm. Except those featherlight touches make me grit my teeth. When she tugs at the elastic, so soft, I almost come in my pants. With a grunt of impatience, I push down my briefs. My cock falls heavy against her hand. The back of her fingers feels cool against the iron brand of me. She whimpers in surprise. Or maybe fear.

Hell, I'm big. But not a monster. If she's scared of my dick, it's because someone hurt her with one. That should be enough to make me stop.

I touch my thumb to her bottom lip, rubbing softly. "Open for me."

God help her, she does. Her lips part. I push my thumb inside. She's wet and warm. My cock throbs, wanting inside. I fist it with my other hand, stroking once, twice. Casual enough to keep me from coming. She waits for what I'm going to do next.

"You're so open. So vulnerable. You know that, don't you? I could do anything to you right now. I could fuck your throat. Block your air until you pass out."

A hitch in her breath. "Do you want to do those things?"

"You would be shocked at the things I want to do to you." I want to tangle in the sheets with her and talk until the early hours of morning. I want to fall in love. That's what's wrong with me, my fatal flaw. The insistent desire to enmesh myself with another human being.

Do I want to fuck her throat?

No, which is why I'm going to do it.

"I'm not sure I can—"

"You can take it," I say, implacable. "Put your hands behind your back."

She moves her hands slowly and clasps them together. I have to clench my teeth to keep from coming. Such undeserved trust. That's her fatal flaw. I shouldn't find it so goddamn beautiful.

I put the head of my cock to her mouth. I'm already slick at the tip from precum, and I slide against her lips, painting them. We're feeling each other in our most sensitive places, learning an intimate terrain. It takes herculean effort to pause and sheathe myself in a condom. Then I push inside. I rest myself on her tongue. She closes around me, her eyes wide, her movements clumsy. It's like she's never done this before.

It's like she's never done this before.

The thought is almost enough to make me stop. Almost.

She might be used to a hand at the back of her head across the gearshift. I'm going to teach her how to do this right so she's not afraid of it. *Yes, ladies and gentlemen, nominate Sutton Mayfair for sainthood. I'm going to show a prostitute how to suck dick.*

"Easy," I tell her. "Slow down. Hold on to the tip, nothing more."

She calms, quiets, holds the tip in her mouth. God, she's incredible like this. I could stare at her for hours, my very own Renoir in the form of a mouth on my cock.

"That's right. That's good." I stroke her hair, the way I'd tame a wild horse. "You feel so good and wet and warm. This is the only place I want to be right now."

Her eyes are liquid gold looking up at me. Slowly, slowly, slowly, she runs her tongue along the crest. I shudder, and she sees her power. I watch the realization dawn in her. A blowjob isn't a form of worship. It's a way to bring me to my knees.

She strokes her tongue in a sweeping circle, her gaze never leaving mine. My responses give her clues. My groan, the forward shift of my hips.

The way I run her hair through my hands, sifting for gold. "Yes. Fucking yes. Right there, sweet thing. I'm yours."

Incoherent. Meaningless. I'm mumbling enough things to expose me, fully, but she only sucks and licks and nuzzles at me through the latex, and I gasp out my gratitude.

Climax builds in my balls. It climbs to the base of my spine. "Hold still," I murmur. "Let me fuck that gorgeous mouth. I won't go too fast. I won't hurt you."

Her tongue goes still. Her mouth opens wider. She strengthens her hold on her hands behind her back. A mumbling sound around the flesh of my cock. Assent.

I hold her head steady with one hand and my cock with the other. The urge to drive deeper tightens my hips. My teeth grind together. Only force of will keeps me slow and even.

"Fuck." I'm halfway in her mouth, already bumping the back of her throat.

She makes a small, desperate sound that is neither refusal nor agreement. It's a sound of fullness that makes my balls tighten.

"A little deeper," I mutter, and push into the resistant flesh, hold myself there for a count of one, two, three, and then pull out. She gasps a fresh breath around my slick cock.

When she's calmed herself I push in again. One, two, three. Again and again, until her lips are swollen and her chin is slick with saliva. She breathes only when I let her, a deep drink of air before I push myself into that snug place once more.

The climax builds to an almost painful pitch, and I hold it back out of stubbornness alone. I want this forever, an eternity, this moment of pure selfish sex without the guilt or recrimination that comes after. My body can't withstand eternity. Her throat presses the orgasm out of me, and I come in rough, uneven thrusts, without any of the care her tender throat needs.

My knees are still weak from coming when I drag her to the couch. Be damned to selfishness and stubbornness. I need to taste her pussy. Need to make her come. Need to have sex the way that feels good to me, and that's with my face between her thighs.

She puts up a startled fight. "Wait. What? I don't—"

"I need to taste you," I say, damn near begging. I don't know what I'll do if she says no. I need the salt sweet on my tongue. I need her velvet folds against my mouth.

"Yes," she breathes, and I let out a whoosh of relief.

I spread her legs, ready to dive in—but I pause to look at her, because I haven't. How backwards this sex is, when it's paid for. Sex first and kissing later. A blowjob first and looking later.

She's pink and pale, like a flower when it's first bloomed. The idea of other men using her, without any appreciation of what they have, makes me sick. Even though I'm one of those men.

I nuzzle against the inside of her thigh, and she gives a breathless, ticklish laugh.

Next comes a gentle bite, a graze of my teeth, because sometimes pleasure hurts. She makes a mewling sound that turns my cock to steel again.

I lick her from the base of her sex to her clit, lingering at the slick nub, swirling it with my tongue, lapping with increasing force until she shudders and jerks and comes. At the end her hands come to tangle in my hair, to hold me still where she wants, and I groan my approval.

Need builds to a fever pitch. I fumble in my pants for another condom, wincing as it slides over my still-slick cock. God, I'm going to ache when this is over, and I won't regret a thing.

She's still swollen from coming, and I press the head of my cock into her pink flesh. She squirms, and I murmur soft words. "It's okay, sweet thing. You can take me."

"Wait," she gasps. "Wait. Wait."

I pause with only an inch of me inside her, gasping at the strain. I want to plunge inside her heat. I want to fuck her hard. Instead I'm held captive in this space, panting. "What is it? I can go slower." I don't know how, but somehow I'll find a way to slow down if that's what she needs. "Is this too fast?"

"No. Go ahead. Do it." Except her voice doesn't sound excited anymore. She sounds strained. Her face is pressed sideways into the couch, and I turn her chin so I can see her eyes. Tears glisten there. *Shit.* I yank myself out of her, ignoring the yowling protest of my dick.

"What the hell is wrong?" Jesus. I force myself to calm the fuck down. "What happened?"

"Nothing. Just do it."

She holds her legs apart so I can—what? Plunge inside without any more foreplay? Fuck her even though she's crying? My insides turn cold. Nothing about her pose looks sexy now.

It just looks like someone trying to please me. Because that's what she is.

SKYE WARREN

My cock is still hard, still hopeful it will get to be inside her, the stupid fuck.

I collapse onto my back next to her on the couch. "Jesus," I mutter. "Someone did a number on you, didn't they? Probably several someones. I'm going to hell for this."

She brings her knees close together and wraps her arms around them. It's a protective pose, and something in my heart cracks at the sight. "I'm sorry."

"Don't be sorry."

"It's just that my first… my last… the one customer I had before you… he wasn't gentle with me. Not like you were. So I don't know why I freaked out like it would be the same."

"You've only had one customer before me?"

She whispers staring straight ahead. "It hurt so bad."

Christ. I want to ask if she was a virgin before that or if she's ever had good sex. What a fucking world to live in, where there are women with no other choices. "I'm the one who's sorry."

"No, what you did… it…" Her cheeks turn the same shade of pink as her pussy. "It felt good."

So tempting. It's so fucking tempting to spread her legs and show her how good it can feel

70

to play with her clit while I pump into her pussy. To fuck her bare and then lick the liquid from her pussy. I want to do so many things with her, but I'm not going to.

It hurt so bad.

Fuck.

CHAPTER EIGHT

SUTTON

I WAKE UP to the sound of Bowie, my rooster. He reminds me I need to check on the goddamn hens. Thankfully I have Whitney who lives in the guesthouse or all the animals would have starved by now. Including me. Even so I've been shirking my duties. Exactly like Dad used to do. Hell.

A faint movement from beside me. Ashleigh becomes still.

"Good morning," I say, forcing a casual voice.

She gives me a cautious glance. "Hi."

Does she think I'm going to kick her out as soon as she opens her eyes? I convinced her to come to my bed only after swearing I wouldn't touch her. And I managed to do that, despite the blue state of my balls. "Sleep well?"

She moves each arm and then each leg, checking that they're all there, as if I might have ravenously eaten a limb overnight. She treats me like I'm a monster, because that's exactly what I taught her I am.

"Breakfast?"

The idea of food loosens her up. A sigh that can almost be called content. She stretches like a cat, long and decadent, with a little shiver at the end. "I *love* breakfast."

"Perfect. I'll make migas."

"Migas? I was thinking like a bagel or something."

"Migas are better than bagels."

She looks skeptical, and I have to laugh. "Fresh eggs from my chickens, onions, garlic, jalapeno. Black pepper and salt. Corn tortillas, cheddar cheese. And my homemade salsa."

"You make your own salsa?"

"It's easy, and a million times better than from the jar."

She still looks uncertain. "I don't think I've ever had a spicy breakfast before."

"I can make it mild. But here's the deal. If you don't love it, we'll find bagels for you."

A flush colors her cheeks. "I mean, of course I'll eat it. And love it. I didn't mean to be demanding. God, I'm so hungry I would eat about anything. I'd eat jalapenos like they were grapes."

The reminder that she lives hand to mouth makes me cold. It's one thing to use her for sex when I'm pissed off and heartbroken. Another thing to see her too skinny body in the light of morning. "Is there someone I can call? A sister? A friend? Someone who can help you get on your feet."

She looks away. Her profile looks stark against the pale light. "No."

"Maybe there's a shelter. Or somewhere that helps women who—"

"*No.*"

"How did you end up doing this?"

"It's none of your business, Sutton. You didn't buy that from me. You bought my body and my time. You paid for my mouth, which you love so much, but you didn't buy my secrets."

Her agitation fills the air around us, a crackling energy that bites at my skin. I stroke her arm, her cheek, the tender side of her neck. "Hey," I whisper. "You're safe with me."

She meets my eyes then, and she looks haunted—it's a look that carves into my soul. One of pain and despair. One I'd do anything in that moment to erase. "Am I?"

"Yes. There will be migas *and* bagels, because

why the hell should we choose? And then…"

"And then?" she asks, resigned, already knowing the answer.

And then she'll go back to the street, to another man to fuck. God. I can't stand the idea. I don't care if that makes me hypocritical and jealous. I can't deal with the idea of someone touching her. And I definitely can't stand the idea of her being hungry. "Listen, I really need a plus-one for this wedding. I don't want to sit alone and deal with everyone's pity."

She lifts an eyebrow. "So you want me to—? God no."

"Why not? You enjoy spending time with me. You know I can make you enjoy it."

"Because I'm a prostitute. Why do I have to spell it out?"

"No one there will know. Even in the off chance they've seen you on the street, they won't put it together. People see what they expect to see."

"What if I *want* them to know?"

"Then tell them. What the hell do I care? Do what you want. Just come with me." I don't know why it's so important to me that she comes. So that I can give her more money? Yes. So that she'll be safe for another night? Yes. There's something else, though, some ineffable sense that I'd be lost without her.

"I don't want them to know," she says on a sigh. "But I don't have a dress."

"Then we'll go shopping." I glance at the alarm clock. "We have enough time to make migas, raid Nordstrom's, and show up on time to the wedding."

"I don't know—"

She wants to. I can tell that much. And I'm suddenly suffused with the desire to see her in something expensive, something comfortable and luxurious and sexy—the very opposite of her cheap satin halter and black mini skirt that are somewhere on the floor of the living room.

I could probably convince her using only my charm. Maybe tell her she's starting to mean something to me, even after only one night. Except that would change the terms. This should be about money.

"Two thousand dollars," I say gently.

She doesn't meet my eyes this time. "Sold."

CHAPTER NINE

ASHLEIGH

H E TAKES ME to a boutique called Steph's in the Heights, a stylish part of the city. There are no racks of clothing. Only a bevy of gorgeous women, smiling, pensive, and sly. It takes me a minute to understand that they're like mannequins showing off the clothes in various poses. A woman in all black shows us to the back.

"Hello, my love," a woman says, giving Sutton a kiss on both cheeks. "Tell me you're doing well and that you've forgotten all about that traitor."

"Hello, Steph. I heard that traitor dropped a small fortune here last week."

A sniff. "Yes, but I didn't even tell her that the navy jumper looked pedestrian."

He grins. "Is it because you care about me?"

"Yes, you foolish cowboy. Now tell me what you've brought me."

"This is Ashleigh. She needs a dress."

"She needs a makeover and a donut. Look how skinny. Don't starve yourself for the men," she tells me. "It's never worth it."

"There will be time for donuts later. We're in a rush."

She gasps. "The wedding. It's today."

"That's right."

"You give me no time. None. What are you, a size two?" Her sentences run together giving me no room to answer. "Never mind. I'll start bringing dresses. We can't waste a single moment, not with men who wait until the last minute."

I stand on a small platform while Sutton lounges on a sofa. Dresses are held under my chin while Steph makes pronouncements. *This color looks like puke. Here, this one, it's like it was made for her. No, I despise it. Throw it away. Why do we have this dress?*

"Perfect," she exclaims over a particular dress with pale blue ruched fabric. "Now, take off these terrible clothes so we can try this one."

She doesn't move from standing next to me. There don't seem to be any dressing rooms, only walls covered in thick crown molding. "Where should I change?"

"Right here," she says, exasperated. "Come

on. Undress. No need to be modest with Steph. Or with Sutton. Sutton appreciates a woman's body, doesn't he?"

"He does," Sutton says from the sofa, his voice sardonic.

"Oh, but I don't—" Embarrassment heats my cheeks. I'm standing on a *pedestal.* Is this what rich people do, undress on pedestals? God. And even worse, I'm not wearing a bra or underwear. I struggle for the words. "I don't have any—Under here, there isn't—I'd be naked."

Neither of them looks particularly shocked by my confession. Sutton isn't shocked because he undressed me last night. He did more than undress me. He lifted my skirt on the sofa and licked between my legs. From the heated look in his bright blue eyes, he's remembering the same thing.

"This is better," Steph says. "We'll need a strapless bra for this dress. And we'll find you silk panties. Stockings and garters. The whole ensemble will be new."

The whole ensemble will be new. How easy that sounds. How alluring.

I wonder if I'd feel new, too.

"No," I say quickly. "That's too much money. We only need a dress for the wedding."

Sutton relents. "Let her use a dressing room, if it helps her feel better."

The expression on Steph's face is uncompromising. It's impossible to tell how old she is. She has a commanding air and sophisticated clothes— a short dress with high, almost military sleeves. But her face is unlined and softly pretty. Her gaze doesn't leave mine. "This wedding," she tells me softly. "Everyone will be looking at Sutton. Everyone will be looking at who he brings. Don't you want to look your best?"

Because they'll be judging him. I may only be a prostitute, but he's right. They don't have to know that. I can look beautiful and wealthy—like them. "Okay," I say, reaching for the hem of my halter top.

The fabric falls to the floor, and then I'm topless in front of Sutton and a stranger. My nipples turn tight under their gazes, one heated, one assessing. Next I push down my black mini skirt. I step out of my heels, too. With the outside of my foot I push the whole thing off the pedestal.

Then it's just me standing there, completely naked—afraid and ashamed and also exhilarated. Those clothes are the only thing that marks me as living on the street. Without them I could be anyone. I could be someone who's never had rough, cruel hands on her. Someone who belongs by Sutton's side.

Steph lifts the pale blue dress and it falls down my body. As soon as it touches my thighs, she says, "No, definitely. All wrong. The blue matches Sutton's eyes, and that's the only excuse I can make. I was distracted by them." She gazes at me, sly. "Aren't his eyes distracting?"

"Yes," I admit, because I'm staring into them right now.

He's watching my body with lazy possession, relaxed on the sofa. It's the kind of relaxed a wild animal would have, coiled in rare repose. His gaze shows all the heat and sensual intent.

Steph holds up another dress to my naked body. "No no no."

And then I'm revealed again. It's an endless covering and reveal, an endless dressing and undressing. Every single time Sutton turns hotter, until it doesn't seem possible that he should feel more turned on. It must be contagious because my own skin starts feeling hot and itchy.

"This is the perfect one," Steph says when she holds up a gold slinky thing.

It's the same thing she says about every one I've tried on. Despite the glittery sheen, the fabric is soft against my heated skin. It's like a caress.

Instead of shouting *no no no*, Steph turns me gently to face away from Sutton—until I'm looking at a large set of mirrors.

The reflection takes my breath away. The gold dress falls perfectly on my body, highlighting curves in a way that feels elemental. My hair looks tousled from so many dresses going over it. The gold brings out natural champagne strands. I look like someone else entirely. A different species than the scared, hungry girl who lives in a sugar factory. I don't look anything like me.

"I love it," I breathe.

Triumph makes Steph look like a general having won a war.

In the mirror, Sutton's expression is arrested—as if I've taken him by surprise. "Yes," he mutters, almost to himself. "She looks incredible. Jesus. No one will recognize her like that."

My heart sinks, because of course they won't.

And of course he worried about that.

Chapter Ten

Sutton

S T. Martins is the oldest church in Tanglewood. It's been through a plague and a flood and a fire—all the Biblical threats. And here it stands in modern, hand-bricked glory. Light shines in every hue through the stained glass windows. Jesus drags his own cross in one of them. He rises from the dead in another.

I wouldn't have expected Harper to get married in a church. It's a little traditional for her. She could have gotten married knee-deep on an endangered coral reef or in zero gravity on a private space plane. Maybe she could have painted the church out of thin air. She eschews everything ordinary. Or at least it seemed that way. Maybe I didn't know her as well as I thought.

Hugo stands in a throng of bridesmaids with his usual charm, making the women blush. He even disarms the men with that grin, the one that invites you to share in some undefined secret, looking old-world debonair in a tailored tux, his black hair in artful disarray.

We have that in common, the ability to make friends in any room. The ability to charm our way through every woman and most of the men. While meaning none of it, feeling nothing.

The relief in his dark eyes, that's real enough. "Thought you might not come."

"I said I would."

He gives a soft huff of laughter, looking away. "You left early last night."

Lust. Anger. They merged into something ugly last night, something that had almost made a young woman the target of my revenge. I could have turned into my father. Maybe I did. "I made an appearance. Same as I'm doing now."

He glances at my tux. "I suppose you visited Mrs. Cheung."

Someone should alert the media. The next diet craze—alcoholism, thanks to the research by Sutton Mayfair. Six weeks of bingeing stripped away every spare centimeter of space, leaving my frame lean and hard. "She didn't appreciate me showing up without an appointment."

"I'm sure she didn't," Hugo says, his voice mild.

He's the one who discovered Mrs. Cheung when we were broke as hell and trying not to look that way. The tailor shop squats between a dumpling house and a Chinese movie theater, mostly hidden by gnarled bamboo plants allowed to run wild.

We can afford Italian designers and bespoke suits now, but we like to remember where we came from.

"She charged me a ridiculous amount of money. And tried to set me up on a date with her niece." She also gave me a rather colorful setdown in Cantonese while she tucked and trimmed my tux yesterday. A small price to pay to appear presentable today.

That's the whole point of this, pretending nothing is wrong. Helping the happy couple get married without knowing they tore me apart.

"Her niece can do better. Did you tell her you're one step away from liver failure?"

"Now, that's a goddamn dirty lie. My father drank for forty years, and his liver was just fine. It was the tree that got in the way of his truck that did him in."

"Your father was a drunk and a bastard. He should have been put down like a rabid animal."

"Funny. Christopher said the same thing

once."

"Well, Christopher is my friend, too. Even if I'm very angry at him."

"Because he had the fucking audacity to fall in love?"

"*Non.* He was in love with her for many years. He only decided to do anything about it when you expressed an interest in her. That's why I'm angry at him."

"Don't be," I say, my voice flat. "I asked her out first to get a reaction from him."

"Then you're both assholes."

"Yes. Only, he's better at it. But you know what? Even knowing that, I wouldn't change a thing."

"You wouldn't?"

"Well, I'd have started drinking sooner. That's the important thing, recognizing where I went wrong. And making up for lost time."

Christopher Bardot and I were business partners first.

We became both friends and enemies. In one night, with the woman we both loved between us, we almost became lovers. He's going to marry that woman, and I have to smile and laugh and pretend like my stomach isn't ripped into shreds.

Something shifts in the air. I feel the change

echo inside me. I turn.

Ashleigh stands there, wearing that pale gold dress, wobbling on cream-colored Louboutins, looking like a lost lamb. If there were any mercy in this world, some priest would come to shield her from sinners like me. Maybe they'd lock her up in a nunnery where no one could touch her, no one could hurt her.

There isn't mercy in this world.

There are only wolves like me, and we love to tear lambs apart.

"Introduce me to your friend," Hugo murmurs as she approaches.

"Don't be an ass," I say, but it's too late. Of course he's going to be an ass. The very specific Hugo Belmont kind of ass that charms women out of their panties.

"*Magnifique*," he says, his hands fluttering around her like butterfly wings. "You look like an angel standing here beneath the stained glass window."

Her cheeks turn pink. "Thank you."

"This is Hugo. My friend." Though the word *friend* feels like an overstatement when he smiles at her and she smiles back. I consider dunking him in the baptismal pool. I want all her smiles. Which is strange. I've never been jealous with my lovers before. Even with Harper and Christopher, I wanted them together. I just wanted to be with them.

Hugo kisses her hand with outsized chivalry, as if they're in royal court in the eighteenth century. "And what is your name? Sutton has been keeping you in hiding, I think."

"We haven't known each other long. I'm Ashleigh."

That earns me a meaningful glance from Hugo. First name only. Ashleigh. Only a small step up from *what do you want my name to be?* "I'm going to leave her with you," I say, a warning in my voice. "During the ceremony. Don't scare her off."

"Me?" Hugo gives a wounded look. "I think you are the scary one between us."

A musical laugh that belongs to Ashleigh. It sounds young and innocent. And I realize that I've never made her laugh. Only Hugo's done that. Jealousy burns my throat.

Blue appears at the front door. He's wearing a tux and a discreet earpiece, which means he's working the wedding. He owns a security company in Tanglewood. We're good friends. More than that, we're brothers. Dear old Dad sired a handful of bastards. Most of them had to grow up with their mothers—or in Blue's case, with a resentful father who knew he'd been cuckolded.

There's sympathy in his pale blue eyes. "We need your help."

Maybe Christopher got cold feet after all. "Where is he?"

"Not him. The bride. Harper's asking for you."

My heart slows to silence for one disbelieving beat. Followed by a rapid rat-tat-tat pulse. She's asking for me, when she picked some other man. I should tell her no. I should tell her to go to hell. *Harper's asking for you.* "Isn't that Avery's job?"

She's the maid of honor. There are also a handful of bridesmaids who can help, surely. I shouldn't even be a guest at this wedding, but somehow I'm the best man. Now this.

Blue gives a slight cough. "She's locked herself in the steeple. Alone. She says the only person she wants to talk to is you. Of course we can break the lock, but—"

"Christ. I'll go."

A featherlight touch on my arm stops me. Ashleigh looks uncertain and painfully brave in the jeweled light of the stained glass window. "Should I come with you?"

Relief whispers through me. I'm going to plunge into cold, black water, and here's this beautiful rope to hold on to, waiting for me to find my way back. She doesn't know what she does to me with her fragile courage and pale skin. I can see the veins at the hollow of her neck. I can see the throb of her pulse. I want to swallow her whole. "Nah. You wait here."

Her peach-tinted lips reveal her intentions before she speaks, and I learn something else, this girl is stubborn. That's even more alluring than her bravery. "It's no trouble. And besides, you might need help."

The realization hits me like a freight train. Two hundred thousand pounds going at the speed of sound. She's trying to protect me. Homeless and battered. She's trying to protect *me.*

I'm humbled in front of her. Destroyed. "Sure," I manage to say without choking on the word. Sure, I'm going to see the woman I love. Sure, I'm bringing the woman I throat fucked last night. Everything is upside down and broken, but sure sure sure. "Come, then."

Blue directs us to a narrow spiral staircase tucked into the northwest corner. The metal rail groans when I climb the steps. It doesn't want to hold my weight. In contrast it's almost silent when Ashleigh follows behind. She's light as a goddamn butterfly.

When I get to the top of the stairs, I find the door wedged open. Through the slit in the door I see a woman in a puffy white dress. She has her back turned to me, her feet slung over the edge of what must be the bell tower. I'm half-surprised she didn't do a fireman's slide down the rope into the congregation. She could play some rock-amped version of the wedding march. Everything about this wedding screams traditional, which isn't Harper—is it? Or maybe I didn't really know her. Maybe I never walked through her metaphorical house, touching the statues and the books.

Harper doesn't move as I step into the small space. We're alone here. I glance back. Ashleigh stops at the threshold, leaning against the doorframe—either reluctant to intrude or wanting to give us privacy. "Hey," I murmur, shoving my hands into my pockets.

She doesn't look at me, but I can see her pretty lips twist in some unnamable emotion—regret? Anger? Guilt? "I'm surprised you came. I thought you wouldn't want to."

"There's a rule about brides. You can't say no to them on their wedding day."

Her hazel eyes are beautiful. Mysterious. "So I

should ask for the moon?"

Part of me knows she's goading me. The other part's ready to be goaded. "I gave you the moon, Harper. You didn't want it. Not from me, anyway."

A sad twist of her lips. "You hate me."

Three words, and I'm undone. "Of course I don't hate you."

Then what's your excuse for fucking Ashleigh like that? A dark voice in my head sounds like my father. Hating Harper wouldn't have been an excuse, but it would have been something. I have no reason for using her like that, no way to redeem myself.

I gently push aside the lace of her wedding train so I can sit on the hand-scraped bench. "And even if I did, that would say more about me than you. You're allowed to love someone else. You're allowed to choose someone else. You deserve to be happy, Harper."

A notch forms between her eyes. "Could I have been happy with you?"

"No." A note of surprise coloring my voice.

It's not the realization that she wouldn't be happy with me that's a surprise. It's the realization that I couldn't have been happy with her. Harper's gorgeous and glamorous and complex.

Everything I thought I wanted in a woman. But she didn't know me. She'd never run her fingers over the metal mane of a horse. She'd never stretched hard enough to shiver in my bed.

That's the woman waiting on the stairs.

I glance back and find her leaning on the railing, a look of sympathy in her liquid brown eyes. God, she's pitying me. I fucked her mouth raw, and she's standing there feeling bad because I love another woman. I really am a bastard.

"Why did you want to see me?" I ask, without breaking eye contact with Ashleigh.

Harper gives a huff of laughter. "I suppose I didn't want to start my marriage with something dark at the core. That's what I told myself. But maybe I thought you would... be with us. Weren't we good together, all three? I was surprised when you didn't join us last night."

Ashleigh's eyes widen in shock. *Weren't we good together, all three?* Yes, that's right. I fucked a woman. I fucked a man. A big part of me wants to do it again. Forever and ever, amen. Except I wouldn't be the one standing in front of the altar. It would be Christopher and Harper, the real couple. And me, the dirty little secret in their bed.

Harper turns and goes still. "You... brought a date."

She doesn't just mean I brought a date to the wedding. I brought a date to the steeple. I brought this woman, whether shield or comfort or both, when facing the woman I lost. "Yes."

"She's very pretty." The words sound assessing. "No wonder you didn't want to play last night. Why didn't you bring her with you? We could have shared."

Fuck no. The response rips through me, primal and violent. No one touches Ashleigh, not even Christopher. Not even Harper. "Be nice."

That earns me a small smile. "I thought you had to say yes to the bride on her wedding day. What if I want a little kiss? It would be a nice present for Christopher."

"No."

Her expression turns speculative. "How long have you been together?"

"A few weeks," Ashleigh says, which is a lie. She's saying it to spare me, so I don't have to explain that I picked her up on the street sixteen hours ago. Or maybe she's saying it to spare herself. Either way, she looks convincing. "It was love at first sight."

Harper blinks, taken aback for a moment. Then she looks at me—searching, searching. For what? Whatever she finds makes her grin, lopsided and unrepentant. "I have a wedding to get to, you guys. What are we waiting for?"

She hops up, almost tripping over her white frothy gown. I lean down to yank lace out of a splintery clutch. On her way out of the steeple, she gives me a sly glance. Then she leans to whisper something to Ashleigh. A second later she's whooshing down the rickety stairs.

I frown at Ashleigh. "What did she say to you?"

"Nothing."

"Ashleigh…"

She pushes up on her toes and gives me a kiss on my cheek, the warm brush of her lips unbearably soft. It feels impulsive and caring. Affectionate, when there should only be filthy sex between us. "Don't worry," she says, her mouth an inch from mine. "I'm not going anywhere. For I have promises to keep."

"And miles to go before I sleep," I say, reciting the poem.

"And miles to go before I sleep."

That's when I realize I'm grasping her wrist. Only intense willpower forces me to let go of her, finger by finger. Then she's skipping down the stairs. I follow her, bemused and hungry, wondering why I'm more focused on getting

Ashleigh naked again than the woman I love walking down the aisle. She's like some addictive substance. The more I have her, the more I want her. The more I *need* her.

Chapter Eleven

Ashleigh

Sutton leads me back to his friend Hugo, the charming man who's now holding a small child. A woman with pale skin and a wild spray of red hair leans against him. She looks like a fairy sprite with a dark satyr. "Hugo told me we had a guest," she says to me, smiling.

My stomach clenches. What would she think of me if she knew the truth? There are so many people here, it feels like at least someone might recognize me. I should probably be struck by lightning for entering a church, except I stopped believing in God a long time ago. My father was a religious man. He donated money. The priest called him a close friend. It stopped feeling like a betrayal when I accepted that it was all make believe, as real as fairy sprites.

"Hi," I say, feeling shy. "I'm Ashleigh."

"Beatrix. You can call me Bea." The child

squirms, and she takes the little girl with a soft clucking sound. "Darling. Won't you relax? Teething," she confides to me. Her friendly manner makes it easy for me to calm down. No one will recognize me.

"I'm sorry. Can I do something to help?" Except Hugo has already produced some half-frozen toy from his suit jacket, and the toddler grabs for it greedily. She sucks on the blue plastic with an expression of intense relief. "Honestly, I need one of those."

Bea laughs. "I think we'll get along fine." She glances at Sutton. "You can go."

A queen couldn't have dismissed someone better. Still, Sutton doesn't leave right away. He turns to me, a notch between his golden brows. "Are you sure you'll be okay?"

He's beautiful. It's like looking up at some old Roman statue made flesh and blood. The fact that he's also kind and smart… how did Harper leave him? The fates always liked to play tricks. "What will you do if I say no?" I murmur. "Insist that I stand next to you at the altar?"

A slow smile. "Maybe so. You don't think the priest would mind, do you?"

"No way," I say, feeling breathless. "I'm sure he'd let me pass out communion, too."

"So you were raised Catholic," he murmurs to himself, and I realize I've let something slip past my defenses. While we were talking—or would that be flirting?—he saw through me.

"Of course," I say with forced nonchalance. "All the good Catholic girls are slutty. We're rebelling against authority and all that."

He frowns. "You aren't slutty."

I turn away, embarrassed and babbling. "Aren't I? It doesn't matter. Shouldn't you be with Christopher already? The ceremony will start without you."

"Hey." When I don't quiet, he lifts my chin so I'm facing him. Stormy blue eyes study me. It feels like he can see right through my secrets, past my religion and my profession, into the broken heart of me. God, the irony. That's what Harper whispered to me. *Don't break his heart again.* Again, because she knows what she and Christopher did to him. I don't have that kind of power, but I think he might break my heart.

He leans down and brushes his lips against mine—once, twice. A third time, which sends sparks of latent pleasure through my limbs. He's going to pull away; I feel the intention in his hold. I'm not ready to release him. I press my mouth fully against his. It's a clumsy, childish kiss, but it's one I'm giving freely. He stills, as if I'm a wild animal. Yes, yes, that's me. A doe. Why are they made so defenseless? All we can do is run. We stand together in unnatural stillness, connected only by the kiss. His breath brushes my skin. When I step back I feel dazed. His hand steadies me.

"Take care of her," he murmurs to Hugo. He leaves without a backward glance.

Slowly I become aware of my surroundings— the large baptismal pool with water gently lapping, the profusion of royal blue calla lilies in elaborate, artistic arrangements. My cheeks heat with embarrassment that they saw our kiss.

Bea's eyebrows are raised, and even though she tries to act casual I can see a faint flush beneath her freckles. "Well," she says, brisk and businesslike. "Shall we find our seats?"

I mumble something incoherent, and Hugo smooths over the moment with that charm of his. "Two beautiful ladies. That's what I usually have. Now, three." He takes the toddler with a swift kiss on her forehead. "I'm a very lucky man. Come, lead the way."

Beatrix takes my arm, and we head down the bustling aisle to find empty seats. An usher waves us forward. As we move sideways to our places, I see someone glance at me and away. Someone else whispers behind their hand. For a cold moment I think there's actually a scarlet letter pinned to my dress, as if they know, they know, they know. That's impossible. It's not me they're whispering about. The realization makes me even colder. It's Sutton. They're whispering and wondering about me because I came with Sutton.

I raise my chin, doing my best to appear worldly and well satisfied.

"That's good," Bea murmurs. "Let them wonder. They're vultures, all of them."

The wood of the pew is smooth, the program crumpled in my hand. This whole thing is too familiar. It might as well be Daddy sitting next to me. Bile rises in my throat. I force it back. The last thing I need is to spew vomit all over the people in front of us. They're wearing Yves Saint Laurent and Versace, for God's sake. "It doesn't feel right that Sutton should be the best man."

"He's really his only friend. Oh, there's Hugo and Blue, but they're really more Sutton's friend than Christopher's. That's what happens when you put ambition before everything."

"It doesn't seem to have hurt him any. Look at this place." It's filled to the brim with rich, beautiful people. They may not be close friends, but they're here.

"They're mostly here for the drama."

"What do they think's going to happen? Sutton won't disrupt Harper's wedding day."

Bea gives a faint smile. "I know that. And you know that. They don't."

I'm not so foolish as to think Sutton's a saint. I can still remember the feel of his cock in my mouth, his hands on my head, guiding me, teaching me. The memory of his mouth between my legs makes me blush. He made me come again and again.

He has his flaws, but he deserves better than to be the sideshow.

The hair on my neck prickles, and I glance up. Sutton's watching me, that unfathomable ocean turbulent across this many pews. His golden beauty looks striking and sun-drenched, especially in contrast to the man he's standing next to. Christopher Bardot, the developer who's turning dilapidated buildings into luxury hotels, condominiums, and retail. He's well known, even to the street trash like me. One of these days my sugar factory will probably turn into a Louis Vuitton store. He looks like a dark god, all black hair and slashes for brows. His tux is immaculate. Silk and wool wouldn't dare be out of alignment on this man. *Weren't we good together, all three?*

Imagining Sutton with Christopher makes my cheeks warm. I've never felt anything when I imagine Ky with one of his customers—not even his special customer. It's only Sutton that makes the fantasy come alive. It's impossible for him to do anything by half. He's such a physical man, a fully feeling one, which is what makes the heartbreak so real.

And he's so damned strong, so self-assured in his masculinity, that he wouldn't give a damn what anyone thinks. Him and Harper and Christopher. Why did he turn them down? Why would he leave them and bring me home? There's no way I could have satisfied him like they would have. Uncertainty makes knots in my stomach. *Don't break his heart again.*

No. No, I couldn't. Whatever he wants of me, it's already his.

Until I leave. Because that part is inevitable. Just like Mr. Monopoly, he'll drive me back to the west side and drop me off. Ky will make me instant noodles, the way I do for him.

"You know," Bea murmurs beside me. "I'm good friends with Harper."

"Oh." Quickly I run through everything I said about her. Did I make her sound awful? I don't actually think she's awful, but no one can deny the pain Sutton's felt.

Bea laughs. "I don't blame her for following her heart. But I also wouldn't blame you for being protective of Sutton. Someone needs to be."

What does that mean? "I thought you said he had a lot of friends."

"Well, he does. But he only lets them get so close. It's always smiles and good times and easy charm. He keeps the hard stuff locked deep inside."

The hard stuff? That wasn't deep inside last night. It was hovering under the surface of his skin. It was control and force and sex. I give a nervous cough. Because this isn't going to last. "I don't want to give you the wrong impression about me. We aren't… serious."

"No? That kiss he gave you looked pretty serious."

"That's what I mean. That's all there is between us. The… physical stuff."

It's her turn to flush. "Sometimes it starts that way. That's how it was with Hugo and me. But when you let someone in, I mean really let someone in, it can never be purely physical."

Purely physical. Is that how I'd describe what happened between us? No. It felt soul-deep.

Searing. I'm not sure that changes anything. "It will be over soon."

"Okay," she says, sounding unconvinced. "Because he hasn't taken his eyes off you."

The wedding song plays its familiar opening strands, and everyone stands. I stand up too, but I don't turn to face the back of the room. Sutton's staring at me, and I'm staring back. We're both caught in this moment, even as a different story plays out in the aisle. A bride and a groom. Sacred vows. Those things have nothing to do with the fiery ice in Sutton's gaze. He makes a thousand carnal promises to me as the people he loves stand before God. *Yes, yes, yes*. That's my answer back. Because I don't want him to hurt. At least that's the story I tell myself. The truth is much more disturbing. The truth is I want to be hurt.

CHAPTER TWELVE

SUTTON

I'M TOO BUSY watching Ashleigh remember what we did last night and blush to worry about the couple being married in front of me. Until I have to hand the fifteen-thousand-dollar ring over to Christopher from my jacket pocket. Until they kiss.

The chemistry is enough to singe me, standing only a few feet away. I have to watch as Christopher cups her beautiful face. I have to watch as Harper's eyes turn damp. He lowers his head, and I'm jealous of her. She reaches to put her hand around his neck, and I'm jealous of him. It tears me up inside, a thousand different blades. I'm jealous of the goddamn air between them. Loving one person is bad enough. Loving two is pure hell.

Loving three would be enough to break me. I can't let myself fall again. That's the only thing

I'm sure enough of as I watch Christopher bend Harper back for a deeper, more passionate kiss.

The audience stands and claps, a riot of joy. I feel numb.

There's a cold hollow where my heart should be. It's a relief, that empty space. Much better than the pain that I'd feel if it were full. I let Avery take my arm and guide me gently down the aisle after the happy couple. One foot in front of the other.

Limos idle outside the church, and I glance back to the crowd, looking for Ashleigh. I don't see her. Avery tugs me inside the car. "You'll see her at the reception," she murmurs.

I glance at her, and it feels like I'm seeing her for the first time.

Avery Miller is something of Tanglewood royalty. She came from old blood, the St. James family, and married Gabriel Miller under a cloud of scandal. Her expression is soft with sympathy. "You did great in there."

A harsh laugh. My amusement abruptly ends. "It wasn't a particularly hard job."

"Wasn't it?" She smooths her satin dress, its royal blue a perfect complement to the flowers inside. Everything perfect for the wedding of the year. The ride seems to pass in a moment. It seems to take an eternity, my eyes hungry for the sight of Ashleigh.

We arrive at the reception before the happy couple.

"Where'd they go?" Avery muses.

A quickie, my mind helpfully supplies. They're probably tumbling about the back of a limo. Maybe even with a professional boudoir photographer to capture a few blessed shots.

I feel blank as I cross the room, *search* the room. There she is.

Ashleigh looks fresh and pretty. She leans against me. "Are you okay?" she murmurs.

"Of course." Except I feel sick.

Everyone's standing around watching me. Normally I don't give a fuck what people think of me. That's from growing up a Mayfair bastard. I'm used to sideways glances while I count out pennies at the grocery store. I'm *not* used to standing in front of five hundred of the most rich and powerful people in the city while they watch to see if I break down.

"Come on," Ashleigh says, tugging me towards a parquet floor.

A band plays a lively tune, which everyone in the room seems determined to ignore. They're hugging the sides of the grand hotel ballroom, whispering and generally looking like they're at a middle school dance. With more expensive clothes.

With Dom Perignon instead of fruit punch.

"Shouldn't we wait for the bride and groom?"

A slow shake of her head. "You and me. Let's dance, Mayfair."

Her hand is warm and real. Enough to bring me back to the world. A step and a twirl. And a smile quirks my lips. "Thank you."

Her brown eyes look bottomless. "I have some experience with people staring at me."

Guilt fills me. "Hell."

"I'm used to it."

"I want to kick anyone's ass who saw you there."

She gives a self-deprecating laugh. "Everyone goes window shopping."

My hands tighten. The thought of her on the streets will never be palatable to me. Wet. Cold. Jesus. "Don't go back."

"Should we move in together?" Her tone is mocking. "I'm not sure we know each other well enough for that. What if I don't like the way you load the dishwasher? What if you have morning breath?"

"I wash dishes by hand. And I definitely get

morning breath."

"This is how Ky feels."

"What?"

"With Mr. Monopoly. He convinces Ky to stay for days at a time. It's harder for him to come back every time, the longer he's away. He gets attached."

I'm getting attached. "Don't go back. Ever."

She laughs suddenly. "Is this like men who say I love you after sex? You're at a wedding, and now you want to get married. Such a romantic."

It isn't a compliment. I just look at her, because I'm not romantic. This isn't a marriage proposal, and she knows that. I want her for one thing. I can't pretend to be a good man, but I'm safer than the assholes driving through the west side.

"Everyone will make fun of you."

"No one will know."

"I know."

"Are you going to laugh at me?"

"Maybe."

"I'll have to get my revenge somehow." I lean down to brush my lips across her cheek. And then lower, across the shadow of her neck. Butter soft. Sweet. "I won't have any mercy on you, Ashleigh. But you don't want mercy, do you?"

CHAPTER THIRTEEN

ASHLEIGH

THREE DANCES LATER we end up tucked into the corner of the ballroom, claiming an entire ten-seat table to ourselves while everyone mills around the center, finally deigning to dance. Two gold-plated appetizer plates are piled high with asparagus and prosciutto and crab puffs. We're seated right outside the kitchen, and we've been using the waiters who leave as our personal buffet.

A meatball and pale liquid look rather plain in an elaborate soup spoon. I tilt my head back and pour it into my mouth. Spices and savory flavor explode on my tongue. There's cumin and pepper—and God, that broth. Definitely fresh ginger.

Immediately I eye the soup spoon that Sutton snagged, and he laughs, handing it over to me. I eat it ravenously, as if I haven't eaten in days, instead of just a few hours. It seems incomprehensible that I lived on two-day-old hot dogs for so long.

Guilt makes my cheeks heat. "I feel bad about all this food. Shouldn't we save some for the other people? Surely they didn't expect us to eat this much."

He nods his head toward the door, where a woman stands holding a miniature, glossy Yorkie. As I watch she feeds him one of the duck lollipops. And another. Another. "Don't be. At least we're people. I don't even think Mopsie was invited."

That makes me giggle. "Maybe I should bring something back for Sugar."

A raised eyebrow. "Sugar?"

"My cat. Well, she's not mine. She lives on the street. Like me."

Another waiter glides through the swinging doors, and Sutton lifts a hand in gentle but inescapable command. "What do you have, good man?"

"Cast iron-seared Wagyu beef with truffle miso," the server says, lowering the silver tray.

"Ah, contraband. Excellent. We'll take six."

The server must be well trained because he doesn't try to protest that we're taking half his platter. Instead he produces a cocktail napkin as we transfer the pieces to my small mountain.

Only when he's gone do I pop a piece into my mouth. The beef is still hot. It falls apart on my tongue, juicy and subtly spiced. My eyes fall closed. A low moan surrounds me, and I realize that it's mine. God. "It's so good," I say, my mouth still full. I swallow and sigh. "Forget an open bar. This is what weddings should have. Food that feels like a religious experience."

Sutton gives me an arrested expression, those blue eyes turning dark.

"Sorry," I say, realizing too slow that a reference to the wedding would make him sad.

"No, I—" He shakes his head, as if breaking a trance. "The way you look when you ate that is the same as you look when you come. Have another one. Have three."

My cheeks heat. I'm suddenly self-conscious. "What? No?"

He lifts a piece to my mouth, insistent. "Another one."

It already smells like heaven. It feels warm against my lips. I open, and he presses the piece inside, the rough tip of his finger brushing against my tongue. I can't help the loud moan.

Shouting. Clapping. A disruption from the

entrance catches my attention. The bride and groom enter to a round of fierce applause. They look like glamorous movie stars. Harper's hair is down in resplendent honey-brown curls. Christopher seems more disheveled than in the church in some slight, unnamable way—as if his hair's been ruffled and then reordered. They are the perfect picture of newly married couple.

Like everyone else in the room I clap, but I turn a worried glance to Sutton—and find him looking at me. He meets my eyes and then drops his gaze to my mouth.

The couple begins their first dance, and the audience settles slightly to watch them. I sit down without an ounce of grace. Now people are standing between me and the dance floor, making it so I can't see; that's fine, though. I can't stand another second of Sutton's intense scrutiny. God, he makes me feel like I'm the only woman in the room.

Sutton sits down more leisurely beside me.

I take a bite of the persimmons with goat cheese and honey, careful not to look at Sutton when I do, certain that I won't make another sexual sound while eating. Ever again.

"I had a cat once," he says, as casual as anything.

That makes me glance at him. "Did you? What was her name?"

"He was a boy. And I called him Tom."

"For tomcat?"

"For Tom and Jerry."

A shadow falls over his handsome face. "He disappeared one day. I wanted to think it was just one of those things. Maybe he fought a cat who was stronger." A harsh laugh. The grooves around his mouth make him seem suddenly older. Harder. "No one likes to think their dad would kill their pet."

A soft gasp. "Did he?"

"I don't know. Probably. He never liked Tom much. And… he shot my dog right in front of me. Lucy was barking. It was late at night. Dad was drunk as shit."

My chest tightens. "I'm so sorry."

"I sat with her until she was gone."

There are no words, so I lean against him, offering him the warmth of my body. He seems so cold. So alone, for a man who has so many friends.

"I think you might know something about shitty dads," he says softly.

A fist clamps around my throat. "How do you know that?"

His voice becomes wry. "A guess. You don't end up on the streets because you're well cared for. And you don't trust men very much. I'm guessing that started early."

I swallow hard. "It wasn't like that at home. No drinking or shooting my pets. I had food and clothes and… a lot of things. Some people would say I'm crazy for leaving."

"Fuck them. They don't know what it was like."

I look at him sideways. "You don't know what it was like either. I might be crazy."

"No one chooses the street corner unless you have no other option."

"I couldn't stay." My breath catches, remembering. He's right about something—I learned not to trust men early in life. My experience on the streets reinforced that, but it didn't start there.

"What did he do?" The question is so offhand that I can almost answer.

"He—" The words won't come out. I look down, ashamed.

"Should I kill him for you? I might enjoy it."

I face him then, my eyes burning. "Thank you."

"For what?"

"Thank you for being—"

"Kind?" A harsh laugh. He runs two fingers across my cheek, capturing a tear on his skin. "God, you're tempting like this. Crying. Except I want to be the one to make you cry. Only me. Cry and beg and scream. Don't mistake me for a good guy, Ashleigh. I'm a bastard. No one knows that better than you."

CHAPTER FOURTEEN

ASHLEIGH

"**Y**OU READY TO go?" he asks, his voice low.

Not really. Leaving means we're one step closer to saying goodbye. But I wouldn't make him stay at the reception longer than he wants to be here. "Let's blow this joint."

"Better to avoid the rush," he says, his tone pragmatic.

Somehow I think the truth has a lot less to do with a post-party traffic jam. "Let me use the restroom."

The line for the ladies' room has already snaked around a column when I get in line. One of the hotel staff points down a curved stairwell. "There's another set of restrooms down there, miss."

"Thanks," I say, flashing him a grateful smile.

I find a much smaller bathroom tucked in the corner of the second floor. After using it I wash my hands and stare at myself in the reflection. I look like the old me, the one with hot water and a good comb, the one who ate fruits and vegetables. I know how quickly I'll turn back into the street-version of me. Always a little dirty, no matter how much I scrub in the cold gas station bathroom. Always a little hungry even when I've just splurged on fast food burgers with Ky.

Which one is the real Ashleigh? I'm not even sure anymore.

I step outside the bathroom, and a body slams me into the wall. Before I can catch my breath I'm pushed into a closet. From the corner of my eyes I see brooms and toilet paper. A closet. I'm in a closet. There's a heavy weight holding me in place, stealing my air. I force a breath, prepared to scream, but a hand clamps down over my mouth.

"I don't think so," comes the voice. "What would Sutton think when he finds you downstairs with another man? Lord knows the man's already been humiliated enough tonight."

I struggle against the body, against the cruel laughter. Nothing. I'm trapped.

"There, I think we understand each other." Slowly he moves his hand off my mouth and leans back into the light, and I can see the blue eyes that look so much like Sutton's. It's my first customer. God. I feel sick. "You acted all innocent with me, but now I see you dancing here with Sutton Mayfair, pretending to be his date. How much is he paying for the girlfriend experience? I didn't know he was that desperate for a woman."

"He's a hundred times better than you." It's the wrong thing to say. I know it, but I can't stop myself, not when I'm faced with this vicious, pathetic jealousy. Sutton stood there proud and strong today. Anyone should be able to see that. The fact that this man would insult him—

A hand grasps my neck. And squeezes. I gasp out a cry—it's not even pain, this sound. Not even fear. It's pure anger right now, and I scrape my fingers down the side of his face, catching blood in my nails.

He screeches, pulling away before lunging for me again, and I know, *this is it,* I've finally done what Ky warned me not to, pushed a man too far. I'll end up buried in a shallow grave made of trash.

I close my eyes, bracing myself for what happens next.

A whoosh of air by my face. A muffled sound. Nothing slams into me. Nothing hurts, except a lingering pain around my neck. I open my eyes to see Sutton in the closet with us, holding the other man off the ground, his legs dangling, his eyes bulging.

Sutton's voice sounds completely ordinary and calm. "Take my wallet out of my coat pocket. The valet ticket's inside. Have them pull the car around."

What's he going to do while I'm gone? "But—"

"Ashleigh."

"Are you going to hurt him?"

"I'm going to have a talk with him."

I don't particularly care about the man making gasping fish noises, but I don't want Sutton to get violent. But I fumble around in Sutton's coat pocket. Something soft brushes my fingertips. A velvet ring box—empty now. Then I find the wallet and rush out of the room.

It takes me five steps to realize I'm holding a thick billfold of cash. I could take the money and run. It's more than he was going to give me. And it's not like he would miss it. God, even if I pawned the wallet, I'd get enough to eat for days.

It shouldn't matter what he thinks of me.

It does.

When I get downstairs I pause for one terrifying moment. The sidewalk leads to a thousand different restaurants and hotels and bars. There are a thousand alleyways to lose myself in. I could disappear in a matter of seconds.

Instead I go to the valet desk and turn over the ticket. "We'd like the car brought around."

✧   ✧   ✧

SUTTON

WHEN I HEAR her footsteps disappear, I take a step back, releasing Mason from my chokehold. He rubs his throat. "Fuck," he says. "I understand wanting to play the hero, but you could take it easy."

"Put your guard up," I say, my voice guttural.

He doesn't understand. "How much are you paying her? I bet you got her for cheap."

He's gotten enough warning. I throw a punch. It lands, solid, on his jaw. The connection feels right on my knuckles. *He called her cheap.* He put his fucking hands on her. I throw another one.

He spits on the ground. "Jesus. Stop. Fuck."

"Stand up." I have a rule about fighting fair. My father had no problem kicking me when I was down. I don't fight often, but when I do, I make sure the other person has a real goddamn chance. It's a point of pride for me, but the idea's eroding fast in the face of this asshole. "Stand *up*."

A knee on the ground. A hand on the wall.

Close enough. I throw another punch, this time low. The impact with his gut makes him wheeze. He retches on the ground while I shake out my fist. It aches in the way that soothes me.

"You don't talk to her. You don't even talk *about* her. Understand?"

He looks up at me from the ground, panting, disbelieving. "You don't know. How is it possible... you don't know? She's a fucking prostitute, Sutton. She's a whore."

The urge to kick him in the stomach almost cripples me. "I know what she is. I know her a lot better than you do, you sick fuck."

"That's what you think." A laugh that sounds unhinged. "I had her before you, you bastard. I had her weeks ago. She was a bad fuck. Scared and jumpy. Is that how you like them?"

He scared her. This is the man of her nightmares, her first client. The realization settles into my bones, and before I can think, I throw a vicious kick to Mason's middle.

His whole body slams against the wall, and he slumps to the floor, spasming.

For the first time in my life I kicked a man when he's down, and it feels... good. That makes my fall complete. I am like my father. I want to do it again and again, until he regrets ever touching her, until he regrets ever *seeing* her.

It's only with force of will that I reach down to haul him up. I slam him against the wall, but he's clearly nowhere near able to fight back at this point. His gaze is unfocused, his mouth drooling. I slam him against the wall until his eyes meet mine.

"You don't know her."

The man has no sense of self-preservation. "She's a—"

"You're mistaken."

He swallows around the pain. "Okay. Okay."

"Say it. You're mistaken."

"I'm mistaken."

It doesn't feel like enough, this admission. I want him to beg for forgiveness at Ashleigh's feet. I want her to refuse. I want her to give me permission to rip his sorry head from his body.

There are a handful of Mayfair bastards in Tanglewood.

Some of them had good childhoods. Some of them didn't.

Some of them are good men. Some of them aren't.

Only one of them do I hate—and that's Mason Smith. When I look at him, I can only see my father. It's wild to think that in some alternate universe we might have been brothers. Real brothers who grow up together, who fight and support and love each other.

Out of hundreds of thousands of men in the city, she had to get him as her first customer.

Mason's always had a cruel streak. It came out when we were in school together. Ironically he had a good mother and a clueless father. He resented me, my existence, and he made my life hell. Not with fists. He always knew I'd beat him in a fair fight. No, he turned his rich friends against me. The teachers. Anyone would believe a good straight A kid over the dirty, angry Sutton Mayfair.

When I leave the closet I wash my hands, because I need to clean them of the bastard stink. The scent of violence and desperation and liquor that never quite leaves, no matter how hard I scrub.

Ashleigh's waiting for me by my car, while the valet chats her up, clearly interested. Anyone would be. I have no doubt that the man in the BMW getting out of his car, the old guy in a tux with his wife—they've all noticed her. The gold dress highlights her smoking body, but her smile is enough to make even the most hardened man believe in a higher power.

The valet says something, and Ashleigh laughs.

Her fear pulsed from the closet. The only thing I felt when I saw her with Mason was rage. Now that I see her with another man, though, I know how easy it would be for her to find someone good for her. Jealousy. That's the name of the seething mass in my chest. Which is fucking stupid, because I have no claims on her. I don't want any claims on her. I don't need to care about someone else who doesn't care about me.

Chapter Fifteen

Ashleigh

THE RIDE HOME is quiet. I see the red marks on his knuckles. It's easy enough to guess some kind of altercation went down. Maybe he sees it as some man poaching in his territory, even if we're only doing this for pretend. For some strange reason it actually makes me excited to think about him fighting for me. It must be an evolutionary instinct that makes me want him to fight a saber-toothed tiger.

At his house, he comes around to open the door for me. That's the thing about Sutton. He's still a gentleman, even when other people aren't watching. A gentleman, even with reddened knuckles.

When he helps me down I keep hold of his hand. I lean down to kiss the bruises and marks, gently. I want to say thank you. He probably didn't do it for me. It was his own pride, but the primal cavewoman inside me doesn't care.

His eyes turn to ocean as he looks down at me, deep and full of secrets.

I walk inside the house and pause, uncertain where to go from here. He probably should have dropped me off on the street corner, but I'm glad he didn't. Besides, he should keep the dress.

When he comes inside, he takes my hand and leads me to the bedroom.

Here. *Here.* It feels right.

I get on my knees, where he wanted me last night, but he stops me this time. He bends his head and presses a kiss to my mouth. I start to turn away—it's too intimate, even though I'd use my tongue on his cock. Our mouths together is the most painfully acute thing.

He coaxes me to bear it, using slow, soft, gentle kisses.

He lays me down on the bed, so careful with me, all of our clothes still on, lying beside me, and I realize this is how it would be if I were with a man in a regular way. The man in the closet used the words *the girlfriend experience.* I think he meant the experience of the man—but this is my experience, pretending to be Sutton's girlfriend, the one who gets his tenderness.

Part of me doesn't want to do this. I'll feel too

much. Not fear anymore. It will be other things. Pleasure feelings. Need feelings. Hope feelings. Every brush of his lips on mine destroys my defenses. He'll reach the exposed-nerve heart of me, and then what? There won't be anything to protect me from wanting more. I'll want more than he's able to give, and I'll be smaller for it.

His lips are merciless, brushing away every doubt and fear. Until I'm exposed to him. This gold dress does nothing to hide me. There are my body and my dreams. He looks down at both with grave concern. "We don't have to do this," he says.

He's paying hundreds of dollars for this. Thousands of dollars.

That's not why I want it. I want it for myself, to know what it would be like.

I turn him over on the bed until I'm leaning over him. The bow tie and jacket are long gone. I move aside the placket hiding the buttons and undo them one at a time. I kiss the hollow of his throat. And lower, to the mat of hair at this chest. And lower, to his sternum, to the place where bone turns to muscle. And lower, to the ridge of his abs.

In the girlfriend experience I can do whatever I want. I can give him a blowjob—but I don't have to. So I kiss my way back up, finding rough patches of skin where he scarred over, finding sensitive shadows in the valleys of his body. When I get back to the top I kiss him full on the mouth.

He groans. "Ashleigh."

"What should I do?" I whisper.

Large hands span my hips, and then I'm perched on top of him. "Ride me."

My whole body flushes hot when I realize what he's asking, when I think about how exposed I'll be. I've never done that before. Maybe that's the point. There won't be any memories attached to it. Looking down at his sapphire blue eyes I think he knows that.

I unbuckle his belt and unzip his pants. There's nothing underneath except hot flesh. No boxers or briefs. The contact of his cock to my hand makes me jump.

"Easy," he says. "It's not going to hurt you. It just wants to make you feel good."

He's the one who reaches for the bedside table and finds a condom. He hands it over and watches as I fumble open the package. I check the label, but there's no directions. The curl of his lips says he finds that amusing. So I do the obvious thing and roll it over the tip. His cock jumps as I stroke my way down, and I realize why women like this. I have power in this position. He's on his back, looking up, at my mercy. It may only be an illusion; lord knows he's strong enough to overpower me in a second if he wants to. Here's this big strong man with bruised knuckles lying still for me. It's like having a wild animal roll over so I can scratch his belly. The impulse over-whelms me, and I run my fingernails over his abs—only lightly, not hard enough to hurt. He hisses a breath. "Yes," he grunts. "More."

It's the encouragement that I need to lower myself onto his waiting cock. I kneel high enough to fit myself over his cock, which looks massive when it's standing up. It *feels* massive when it's notched at my entrance. I shiver a little, but he does absolutely nothing—he doesn't move his hips up, he doesn't pull mine down. He reaches up to hold the bars of the bed, as if to prove he'll go at my pace. The sight of him like that, stretched out and at my mercy, makes my pussy clench around him. He feels it; he groans.

I press myself down, inch by inch, straining. He moves his hand to the base of his cock, and when I fully impale myself, his thumb waits for my clit. So full. Too full. Except that I rock forward, his thumb's there. It feels good enough that I do it again. And again.

My lids lower. "Can you come like this?"

"I don't fucking care," he grits out, watching me rock above him.

And I realize he's telling the truth. This is a man who gets turned on from watching me come. He genuinely wants this to feel good for me, because that's what gets him off. That releases the valve of worry and doubt until I can finally let loose. I rock and rock against his thumb, closing my eyes to the ecstasy, unabashed in my nakedness, until I come in hard, blinding spasms.

He roars from underneath me, grasping my hips, clasping me hard enough to leave marks, his cock pulsing inside me, holding tight, extending my orgasm as he rides through his own.

Chapter Sixteen

Ashleigh

W E SPEND THREE days and three nights in this strange cocoon of sex and affection. The most surprising part is how much I find myself sharing. Not about Daddy. That part's still too raw. I tell him about Mama and how close we were.

"She had such big dreams for me. She used to say—you can be anything. An astronaut or a race car driver. The President of the United States. And I'd say, I want to be a doctor. There was no doubt in her voice at all. *Then that's what you'll be,* she said."

"You can still do that," he murmurs, stroking my hair.

I nuzzle against his chest, feeling unaccountably safe. We're from different worlds. He owns this ranch and a truck. There are mentions of a business with buildings and investments. I own

what I can carry, and whatever dead animals
Sugar brings me. "I might as well imagine being
an astronaut. Or the President. It's never going to
happen."

"It can," he insists. "You don't have to know
how your dreams will happen to believe in them."

"No one wants their doctor to be a prostitute."

"It's none of their goddamn business. You're
not the only person who's fallen on hard times.
Maybe your family doctor survived the only way
they could. It's not something they advertise on
the door of their clinic."

It's hard to imagine that Dr. Lim ever fell on
hard times. But I wouldn't know, would I? Maybe
he's right. Maybe I don't have to know *how* the
dreams will come true. It's enough to believe.

On the fourth morning he takes me out to the
stables to meet the horses. Stormy and Lickety
Split and Mischief—"be careful, she bites." We
get to the last stall, where a placid-looking mare
stares at me from between a heavy fall of straw-
colored bangs.

"Her name's Haven. Calm and steady."

"She's beautiful."

"You're going to ride her."

I take a step back. "Oh no I'm not."

"Yes, you are."

"I don't know how to ride a horse."

"I'll teach you."

"That seems like something that's going to take…" Longer than we have. How many days are we going to live in this cocoon? It reminds me of what the man said at the wedding reception. The girlfriend experience. That must be what we're having right now. "Too long."

"It'll take the right amount of time. There's no rush."

I glare at him. "Did it ever occur to you that I don't want to ride a horse?"

"No," he says equably. "Everyone wants to ride horses."

Ugh, I hate that he's right. I'm a regular girl who loved ponies when I was younger. All of these horses look strong and beautiful. Emphasis on strong. Their muscles bulge from beneath their glossy coats. They'll probably buck me off if I even try to get in the saddle.

They're also very tall. "How would I even get up there?"

He grins, knowing he's won. "You'll step on my hands."

"I'm going to fall off."

"The most important thing about riding is

that you have to trust the horse."

"I thought the horse should trust me."

"Absolutely, but that's only going to happen if you trust her first."

I make a face at him, because the idea of trusting an animal that much larger and stronger than me makes me cringe. "I'm pretty sure I've already failed the lesson."

A low laugh. "She's more scared of you than you are of her. You're going to ask her to do scary things like walk into water or jump over something. She has to know you'll keep her safe."

"I'm definitely not asking her to jump over anything. No jumping allowed." I study the beautiful gray dappled mare, trying to see fear in her placid eyes. Nope, nothing. "Shouldn't she do what I say? I thought that's the point of the reins."

"Only if you want her afraid. That means backing away or jumping too late."

"How will she even know if I trust her? Will we do trust exercises?"

"Yes." He produces a shiny red apple from his pocket and hands it to me. "Hold this on your palm with your hand flat. Don't curl your fingers."

"She's going to bite me," I warn, but I put out

the apple anyway. The mare snuffles at my hand without taking the treat. She dips her head to considers the apple from the side. For a second it feels like she's going to refuse the offer, and disappointment sinks in my stomach.

Then finally she takes it with a heavy bottom lip.

She crunches the fruit in a few slow chews, and the majesty of her clenches my throat.

"Wow," I breathe.

"She's a beauty," he agrees, not taking his eyes off me.

"Why wouldn't she trust me? Has she been mistreated?"

"It's too fucking common. A handler can be gentle or rough, respect a horse or run her into the ground. A horse will keep going until she falls over dead if you don't stop her." She watches me from her dark eye, as if saying, *that's right. I would do that.*

"That's horrible."

"It's a big responsibility, having a horse."

"How many do you have?"

"Right now? Ten."

Ten animals who would run themselves into the ground for him. Ten who would fall over dead if he doesn't stop them. "So you like responsibility."

He laughs. "I like horses. The responsibility is the price you pay."

The price he pays, like the money he pays me. It seems all of the things he enjoys cost him something. That's a small consolation, because the things he enjoys cost me everything. "Can I ride her?"

He leans down and laces his hands together. "Step up this way. Grab the horn on the saddle and swing your leg over."

I swing hard enough that I almost fall over the other side but I right myself. She feels a lot taller when I'm on top of her than when I was on the ground.

When I'm seated, he says, "Don't worry about telling her anything. She knows how to walk and where to go. Remember. You've got to trust her."

Haven takes a step forward, and I jolt in the saddle. Another, and I almost fall out. On the third step I move my hips at the right moment. Only then do I understand what he means by trust. I have to move with her. This isn't about being carried around. I'm not a passenger. This is an active form of trust, one that requires me to become part of her.

She moves into an easy gait, and I laugh in

exhilaration.

Sutton makes a whistling sound, and the bay moves toward him. Haven stops in front of him, and he walks to the side of her. He reaches his hands up, circling my hips and helping me down. The ground feels unsteady after being on the horse for only a few minutes.

He'd been smiling before, but now he looks serious. "What happened to you?"

He means before I ended up on the street. My throat tightens. "My secrets are my own."

"Ashleigh—"

"My little horse must think it queer," I say. It's a cheap shot, a feint so that he'll stop asking what I'm not going to answer. "To stop without a farmhouse near."

He's everything stern and hard and frustrated, but he still completes the verse of the Robert Frost poem. "Between the woods and the frozen lake. The darkest evening of the year."

Chapter Seventeen

Ashleigh

T HE AFTERNOON GIVES way to dusk. I wake up with a contentment written on my bones. I want to lie in this bed forever—and that terrifies me. This isn't my bed or my house. I belong on the streets. Being comfortable here will only make it harder there.

Sutton slumbers next to me, a heavy mass of muscle and heartbreak. He doesn't stir even when I slip from the bed. He reached for me so many times, had sex with me in so many different positions. Somehow I liked every single one of them. He made me come so hard I saw lights behind my eyes. I didn't know that would be possible. Not for any woman; definitely not for me.

I look at the bristles on his cheek and the curve of his ear. He's not mine.

I'm a substitute for the bodies he'd rather be

fucking.

In the living room I find his phone, which isn't locked. I order an Uber that's fifteen minutes away. And I dig into his wallet for the money he promised.

Thirty minutes.

That's how long it takes from my last glimpse of Sutton to the first sight of the sugar factory.

"Ky?" The word echoes back to me. He doesn't usually go out so early.

Sugar gives me an imperious meow that shames me for how long I've been gone. There are three different rat carcasses, each torn open and buzzing with flies. My stomach turns over. What a way to come home. *This isn't home.* No. Sutton's house is a home. This is a sad parody.

I climb the roof. "Ky?"

Nothing.

Maybe he went out early to look for a customer. Except he doesn't usually go out when he's flush with money. Maybe Mr. Monopoly came back for another round. Except he usually only comes once a month. The back of my neck prickles with warning. Ky could be anywhere in the city, perfectly safe.

It doesn't feel right.

I head back down to the street, determined to

find him. There's a club a few streets over. Well, it's more of a warehouse with bass. Sometimes Ky comes back from there smelling like pot.

The bouncer stops me, giving me an interested full-body glance. "You working?"

My cheeks flush. He's made no secret that he wants to fuck me. And that he's willing to pay. Which means it's just that obvious what I am. God, my hair's still bed-rumpled. I probably smell like sex.

"Not tonight," I manage to say, hoping I sound casual about it.

He doesn't move from the middle of the door. "How bad you want to get in?"

Oh God. Is he going to make me do something with him? He must sense my desperation, because I really do need to get into the club. It's the only place I know where Ky might be, and every instinct I have is screaming that he needs help. "Bad," I whisper.

"Let me see your tits."

My skin prickles into goose bumps. I feel hot all over and then freezing cold. "My—"

"I just want to see them. That's all."

I stare at this man, who would have seemed handsome in any other context. He's clearly muscled and well groomed. He could have a woman the regular way, couldn't he? I don't even know what the regular way is. Champagne glasses and little Yorkies eating Wagyu beef? That isn't normal.

My stomach clenches, and I glance to the alley.

"Nah," he says, reading my thoughts. "It's too dark to see. Besides, if I got you back there, I'd want to do more than look." His voice turns gentle, coaxing. "All I want is a little glance."

Trembles run through my arms like little earthquakes. I reach for the hem of my emerald green shirt and lift—slow, slow, slow. I'm not wearing a bra. Then my breasts are exposed to the night air.

He sucks in a breath. "Yeah." His voice sounds thicker. "Those are nice."

I stare straight ahead, at the patch of black fabric on his shirt, not meeting his eyes. I start to lower my shirt but he stops me with a rough sound. "A little longer, baby girl."

It feels like I'm someone else, watching this woman lift her shirt for a stranger. Standing in the street where anyone who turns the corner could see. Of course no one will turn this corner. It's a rough part of town and an illegal club. On a Tuesday. Which means he could drag me into a corner and—

A rough palm cups my breast, and I jump. "You said you were only looking."

"Calm down," he says with a pointed squeeze. "One touch. Not like I'm the first one."

"But you said—" Tears prick the back of my eyes, and I feel foolish for believing him. Or for believing anyone. Isn't the world full of liars? I learned that early. How could I forget?

He squeezes my nipple, and pleasure shoots through my body. I feel sick. Horrified. How could this feel good? Only now do I understand how thoroughly Sutton has ruined me. Before this I didn't know what great sex was like. My body had no idea that pressure on my nipples led to orgasms. There's no way that I could come for this man—I feel cold inside. But my body doesn't know that. It's well trained by Sutton's mouth and hands. By his cock.

This is what Ky meant when he said it was harder to come back. It wasn't about the soft bed or the great food. It was about the sex—because Sutton made it feel real. I bet Mr. Monopoly does that, too.

The bouncer's hand drops. He gives me a nod that I interpret as, *Go ahead and cover your tits.*

I shove down my shirt, feeling queasy with

humiliation.

"You come see me later," he says, still sounding turned on. "I got paid yesterday, and I'd love a round with you. I'll take it easy, I promise. Won't rough you up or anything."

He doesn't wait for a response but stands to the side, and tears climb down my cheeks as I duck my head and brush past him. Strobe lights and heavy bass hit me like a fist. I wipe my face with my arms. Bodies are draped across dirty cushions on the floor, most of the people already stoned out of their minds even though it's still early. I suppose anyone who needs to work tonight will show up later. These people are the ones who already earned their money the night before.

I search through them, wondering if I'd even recognize Ky with the distorted lights. Breaks in the music reveal moans and rhythmic thumps. Someone's having sex in one of these corners.

Deep in the back I finally find Ky. He's by himself—or as close as you can come in this place. Somehow he's got a two-seater couch to himself. There are track marks on his open arm. His mouth is open, as if he's sleeping. Except he's not. His eyes are open.

He's dead.

For a terrible moment he seems dead—cold and clammy and unmoving. Then his eyes focus on me, and he snaps alert. "Ashleigh. Hell. *Hell.* I thought you were dead."

I'm almost hysterical with worry, with the emotional seesaw of seeing him this way and wondering if he'd overdosed before I could find him. "I thought *you* were dead, you big dummy."

That makes him laugh, a wild and raucous sound. He's high as a kite. "When you didn't come home for two nights I thought some sick fuck had driven you out to the woods and killed you."

"So you decided to come spend all your money on a freaking needle?"

He squints at me. "Were you in the woods?"

"Close enough," I say on a sigh. "Come on. Let's get you home. You're going to feel like shit tomorrow. And you won't get any sympathy from me. I'm the one who's gotta clean up the rats."

Chapter Eighteen

Sutton

I WAKE UP in the middle of the night with a start, becoming aware in an instant, certain that I'm alone in the house. My heart's made of lead while I check the bathroom, the kitchen, even the goddamn front porch, as if she might be swinging with her toes on the scarred wooden boards. Even the crickets are quiet at this hour. The world feels ungodly silent. I step out into the grass and look up, wearing jeans and nothing else. The dark sky leans down on me, as if filled with water, heavy and threatening.

When I go back inside I find my phone on the breakfast table, set neatly beside my wallet, and a note written on a Post-it. *I took the money you promised.* It continues on the back. *Left some for Uber.* I stare at the loops as if her handwriting can somehow tell me about her soul.

Why the hell do I want to know about her

soul? I don't. I wanted sex from her and I got that. Plenty of sex. A truly ridiculous amount of sex. I climaxed so hard I had a goddamn stroke.

The only reason I feel bereft now is… that I'd have given her a bonus. It's not nearly enough money, what I promised, what she took. And I'd have given her a ride back myself. The whole thing would have felt demeaning and cheap, but hell. It's not like waking up sad is any better.

"Why didn't you wake me up, Ashleigh?"

The Post-it note doesn't answer.

Because she didn't want to say goodbye, asshole. This isn't the standard morning after. This is a paid service. Except I know she didn't think of it like that. I didn't, either.

I grab the wallet and keys and shove them in my pocket. I'll go after her. The app says she was dropped off at the Den, but I should check on her. I should make sure she's okay. I should…

I should leave her the hell alone. Jesus.

When would it end? Never. I'd pretend I was doing it to help her, but in reality I'd just install her in my house as my personal sex slave. I'd be the laughingstock of Tanglewood, like she said, but I don't give a shit about that. I swore I'd never be like my father. Panting after Christopher. After Harper. Now Ashleigh. Do I fall in love every six goddamn months? I always knew he fucked a lot of women. I never realized that he may have actually loved them all.

Slowly I pull the wallet and keys out of my pocket. Toss them onto the table.

I'm not goddamn Mother Teresa to help people on the street. And I'm not going to be a man who takes advantage of her. That leaves me with no rights to her whatsoever.

"Fuck," I mutter, running a hand over my face.

The irony is that there are only two people I could talk to about this who'd understand. Both of those people are currently on their honeymoon in Bali.

I wonder what Harper told her in the steeple. *Don't think about Ashleigh.*

The sun exhales a dim light for hours before dawn. I walk the length of my fence in boots and jeans, no shirt, trying to connect with the land. I used to love every blade of grass, every grain of dirt. Every molecule of air. I still do, but it feels a little emptier somehow. As if Ashleigh gave a piece of herself to the trees and the animals and the earth. Now that she's gone, they don't know what to do.

High-pitched squealing tells me that it's feeding time.

I catch my sister as she's coming out of the pigpen. There are at least six Mayfair bastards in Tanglewood—men with that inherited anger and blue eyes. Whitney's the only girl that we know about. She came to live on the ranch a few years ago. A straw hat sits on her head, ready to shield her freckles when the sun comes out. "She leave?" she asks.

"Did who leave?"

A snort. She heads back to the barn, and I follow at a slower pace, feeling like a lazy bum. The fact that I pay Whitney well doesn't make it any better. "You've been holed up at the house with someone."

I watch as she prepares the large bottle for the calf. "Someone underweight?"

Sometimes a calf needs to supplement nursing with the bottle. "Chess won't tolerate it."

"Hell. Let me talk to her." Chess is a finicky cow, but I can get her to nurse. She'll kick and bite, until I stroke her gently, until I coax her to let the calf drink. She's got the milk already. It'll make her feel better to let it go.

"You were busy with your guest, and I figured that was fine, considering the timing. Besides, it won't hurt the calf to drink from the bottle."

"Give me a minute. I'll get her out of the stall and—"

"Don't." Those blue eyes flash, a mirror image of mine. "Not everyone wants to be a mom, Sutton. You should know that as well as anyone. So don't bother convincing her of anything."

I wait while Whitney fills the bottle and puts on a large nipple. There's formula, if we needed it, but Chess has never minded humans handling her. It's the calves she minds.

When we get to the pen I corral the calf myself. It's my way of saying sorry for whatever the hell I did to piss off Whitney. The calf vibrates in my hold, whether from excitement or fear, I don't know. "Shhhh," I say, making the same sounds I'd make for Chess. I run one hand along her flank. "You're okay."

Whitney doesn't meet my eyes as she bottle-feeds.

"Are you going to tell me why you're ornery?"

That upturned nose and wide eyes make her look young, even if her hands are chapped from hard work. She looks as young as she did when we were both in grade school. She had a crush on me, back then. Until someone finally clued her in that we were most likely step-siblings. Then she got so embarrassed she didn't speak to me for a year. We reconnected as adults, and she takes to the horses as well as me.

"I'm not jealous," she finally says.

"Well. Okay then."

"I'm wondering about this girl, though. If she knows that you're… unavailable."

"You mean, does she know I'm in love with someone else?" Two other people, to be exact. Most people don't know about Christopher, though. Only Harper. "She knows. She came to the wedding with me."

"It's still fucked up that he asked you to be his best man."

"It wasn't as bad as I thought it would be." Because Ashleigh was with me. She was like my guardian angel, appearing when I needed her and then disappearing. Gone, gone, gone. So it's just my bad luck that I didn't stop needing her when she left.

Chapter Nineteen

Sutton

THE NEXT MORNING I find myself getting dressed the way I used to—in a suit. I head into the small offices of Mayfair Building Co, where I busted my ass on construction projects. That was before I met Christopher. Before I partnered with him and fell in love.

Our joint company, Bardot and Mayfair, had slick offices in a high-rise. It's now empty. Winning Harper meant more than just a stumble in our friendship. He didn't want to go to work every day with the man she'd fucked—and maybe loved, for half a second there.

Christopher went to work on a hotel that we'd planned to build together.

He's been working, while I've been drinking and fucking.

For some reason, it seems that today, the day after Ashleigh left me, that's going to change. A stack of mail piles up on the leather top of my desk. I'm sure it's a good deal worse in my email inbox. Without any pomp or circumstance, I sit down and get to work. I'm halfway through the stack of correspondence when my secretary comes in.

"Sutton Mayfair. You could have called, you know? Nearly gave me a heart attack. You don't come in for weeks, *weeks*, and then one day you're sitting at your desk as if you never left."

That makes me grin. "I'm sorry, Mrs. Ness."

"And you've lost weight. What have you been eating? Your color's not good either."

The list of my shortcomings goes on for some time, but I take it with the certainty that I'm back where I belong. Mrs. Ness is one of the many women my father loved and left. I suppose it's awkward, me hiring her. There are a lot of awkward moments in life when your father's fucked half the female population. In Mrs. Ness's case, her husband came back from his military tour, found out about the affair, and kicked her out of the house. It was a scandal when I was in middle school, considering she was the principal.

I probably shouldn't say anything.

That's what I tell myself while she runs through the list of things I should eat and drink, vitamins she's heard are good, essential oils that would help.

"Mrs. Ness."

"Your coffee! How could I forget. I assume you want it the same way—"

"In a moment. I want to ask you something, but I might be overstepping. In fact, I'm definitely overstepping. You can tell me to mind my own business."

She raises her eyebrow in a way that only principals can do. She's never lost the ability, even though she was fired shortly after the affair came out. Things like that were frowned upon twenty years ago. A woman's personal life could keep her from a good job. "Go on."

"With my father. Did you love him?"

"Oh God no. What made you think that? He was such fun though."

A sharp laugh escapes me. "I never saw that side of him."

"No, I suppose you didn't." She gives me a hard look. "I knew he was rough on you. Maybe I didn't realize how rough. Or maybe I didn't want to know, because I couldn't have been with him, then."

"I'm not looking for sympathy."

She scoffs. "Of course not. Sutton Mayfair

wouldn't ever want sympathy. You don't have a lot in common with your father, but you came by that pride honest."

"This is why I keep you on payroll, Mrs. Ness. You flatter me."

"You keep me around as penance. Don't think I don't know. I don't mind, though. Someone has to remind you to eat. Now what made you ask about your father after all this time?"

"I suppose I just wondered… if any of it was real."

"Then you're asking the wrong question. Was it real? Of course it was. I was married to a man who let his fists do the talking, but I got to experience a passionate affair. That's real."

"I'm sorry," I murmur. "For bringing it up. For stirring up old memories."

"Your father was good to me. Real good. He saved the bad for you, I think."

My stomach clenches, remembering the beatings and the hunger. The certainty that I would die before I got old enough to leave. "Yeah. I think so, too."

"Now you swallow your pride and check your email."

A bark of laughter. "Yes, ma'am."

The call comes an hour later from Blue. His security company runs, among other things, private investigations. I didn't want to work with my assigned guy, no matter how skilled he is. This is personal, so I asked Blue to look into it.

"I have the information you asked for."

I close the door of my office. "Go ahead."

"Ashleigh Barnes, reported missing six months ago by her father, Jebediah Barnes. Straight A student before that, family and friends insist that she'd never run away."

Straight A student. My stomach clenches. "Age."

"Seventeen."

My heart pounds in my ears, my chest. I can feel it pounding in my fucking eyes. Seventeen. Seventeen? I want to throw my fist into the wall. Or break down on my office floor and cry. I have to do something with this knowledge. Blue's voice comes through the phone, sounding a million miles away. He's saying something about the age of consent being sixteen and not being on trial for statutory charges, because he's a smart guy—he knows why I'm asking. Jesus. I'm not worried about going to jail. Someone *should* put me there. Throw away the key. I don't care what the law says. She was too young for me in every way.

Chapter Twenty

Ashleigh

KY'S NOT OKAY.

His breathing is shallow. We've still got the money from Sutton, but I don't know if I can even get him into the urgent care. He can't walk or even move. He's barely conscious. I can go down to the gas station and call an ambulance, but they're not going to take the cash in my pocket. They want a credit card.

He moans and strains his head back. Once they calm him down they'll probably charge him for using. And maybe throw in a solicitation charge.

"Hush," I whisper, pressing the cool compress to his forehead. I wish I knew what the problem was. Is it the crack? He should have come down by now. I'm not sure what kind of side effects can happen. I've seen him come back high before; it's never been like this.

"Ash," he mumbles. "Ash. *Ash.*"

I clench his hand. "I'm right here. Can't you see me?"

He looks right through me. "I'm dying, Ashleigh."

"Don't say that. Don't you dare say that. You kept me alive. You know that. You found me in that alley, and I was ready to give up, and you kept me alive. Now I'm returning the favor."

"Can't—"

"You can. Now I'm going to get more ice. You wait here and rest."

When I'm around the corner, when he can't see me, I stop and put my fists to my eyes. I can't afford to cry right now. I have to figure out what to do for Ky. More ice isn't going to help.

There's a doctor in the west wide. I've heard about him. He takes cash or trade, whatever you can afford. I have no idea how to find him, but I'll start at the club. Maybe the bouncer will trade the information for looking at my tits again. The thought sickens me, but I'll do anything.

I clamber over the sill of a broken window and climb down the fire escape. When I reach the bottom rung I let my body hang loose. And let go. I fall to the ground.

"Hello, Ashleigh."

With a shriek of surprise I whirl. It's Sutton. Not the Sutton I recognize from the rumpled bed, his jaw unshaven, his hair a mess of curls. This Sutton is wearing a suit. He looks buttoned-up and proper, even more so than the night of the bachelor party.

"You're seventeen," he says.

I stare at him, shocked out of my worry for a full second. "How old did you think I am?"

"Eighteen. At least."

A strange laugh fills the air. It's mine. "I turn eighteen in a few months. Do you want me to look you up then? Because I don't have time to do *that* right now."

"Do you think I came here to have sex with you?"

"Why else would you find me?" I brush past him. "It doesn't matter what you want right now. I have to do something—I have to—It doesn't matter. I can't talk right now."

He takes my arm. "Hey." And then gentler. "Hey. What's wrong?"

"It's Ky. He's not—" My voice breaks. "He went to a club last night and smoked some bad shit. And it's my fault, because he was worried about me. Now he's not coming down, and I don't know what to do. He's burning up, and he's not even fully *there*."

"Let me help you, Ashleigh. Let me see him."

I stare at him, uncomprehending. Why would he want to help me? Fuck me. Use me. Pay me. That's the relationship we have. Except he asked permission to see Ky. He didn't demand or assume he'd be allowed. He's treating this burnt sugar factory like my actual house.

"Okay," I whisper.

As soon as I take him upstairs, Sutton swears under his breath. He kneels by Ky's side and touches his forehead gently. Ky's still wearing his rentboy clothes, a long hoodie over a mesh tank top, and jeans that dip low. It's a sharp contrast to Sutton's buttoned-up appearance, and it makes Ky look incredibly young. He's so knowledgeable, so world-weary, that it was easy to forget he's younger than me. He should be worrying about a math final or who he's going to ask to homecoming—not sauntering over to rolled-down windows.

"How long has he been like this?"

"I don't know." It feels like an eternity but there aren't clocks in the factory. Not working ones, anyway. I read the time same way a farmer does—by the shades of the sky. "I found him at the club when I got back. At first he seemed like he was flying, you know? Like so high. I got him back here, and tried to sleep it off, but then he started shaking and shivering."

"He needs to be in a hospital. I'm thinking what he got was contaminated, but it could be anything. It's not like there's an FDA for crack cocaine."

My words come out at a whisper. "I'm surprised you know what it was."

"It comes through the country, mostly. People want to blame Colombia or Mexico, but it's Americans who import it and sell it on the streets."

"There's a doctor on the west side." I pull the money I took from his wallet out from under my bed. "They say he takes cash or trade. I have to find him—"

"Anders Sorenson. I know him."

"Oh thank God. Where can I find him?"

He gives me a sharp look. "You're not alone anymore, Ashleigh."

I swallow hard, not even sure what that would look like. "What does that mean?"

"It means we'll take him to the Den. They'll have a bed we can use while we wait for Anders. God knows this heat isn't doing him any favors. It means you can put that money away, because you won't need it, not for this."

"So I'm supposed to rely on you? Don't pretend you're doing this out of the goodness of your heart. This is going to cost me something. I'd rather know up-front."

The belligerence of my words only seems to soften him. "I deserve that, because I was your customer first. When I should have protected you, should have helped you. I can't make up for that. God knows, I'll never be able to. But I'm not your customer anymore. I'm your friend."

I swallow hard. It would sound strange and pathetic to say that I want him to be more than friends. I want him to help me with Ky, and then I want him to take me back to his bed, where everything feels right. "My friend?"

"I can be a friend."

I've seen what he sacrificed for Christopher and Harper—his own happiness. He can be more than a good friend. He can be the very best friend someone could want.

Chapter Twenty-One

Ashleigh

Anders Sorenson is a man with an exceptionally stern expression, with pale hair, high cheekbones, and wintry, pale blue eyes. He sets up a makeshift triage room in the second floor of the Den that could rival any actual hospital room. In short order, without judgment, Ky is hooked up to an IV. The diagnosis includes big words such as tachycardia, hypertension, and coronary vasospasm.

"To put it in layman's terms," he says to me. "Crack cocaine significantly increases the rate of oxygen usage in the body. There's a possibility here of a seizure, a coronary event. Sudden death becomes more likely the higher the hyperthermia."

Sutton makes a growling sound. "Those aren't layman's terms."

"He's having a very bad trip," Anders says.

"What can we do for him?" I'm sitting by his side, holding his hand, which feels clammy and burning hot. His eyelids flutter, but he doesn't seem aware of where he is.

"Exactly what you're doing right now. Hold his hand, talk to him. Try to keep him calm. I'll be watching him closely, including hooking him up to an EKG so I can monitor it."

"Thank you," I say, feeling feverish myself.

"She needs to rest," Sutton says, his voice curt.

Anders gives me an impersonal, assessing look. "You've stayed up with him all night? It won't do him any good to burn yourself out. I can show you to another room."

"I'm not leaving his side." The thought of him waking up in a strange place is enough to make me itchy. Ky acts like nothing bothers him, but I know that would be terrifying.

A nod. "Then you can sleep here in a chair. Or climb into bed with him. It won't hurt him any. Might even calm him. But if he wakes up and acts aggressive, you back away immediately."

"He wouldn't hurt me," I say immediately.

"People do crazy things while under the influence," Anders says, sounding faintly apologetic. "I don't think he'll want to hurt you, but he might not be able to stop himself."

He leaves the room, and I'm left with only the harsh breathing of Ky and the intense presence of Sutton behind me. *I don't think he'll want to hurt you, but he might not be able to stop himself.* I think it's more about Sutton, that statement.

✧　✧　✧

ASHLEIGH

I KEEP VIGIL over Ky while he sleeps, feeling sick that I let him worry for me. We're supposed to stick together. He saved me. Why couldn't I protect him?

"It's not your fault, you know," comes a voice from behind me. A woman walks in wearing jeans and a Henley, her exuberant blonde curls a contradiction to her casual clothes.

"Penny," she says by way of introduction. "My mom named me Penelope from the Odyssey which I've always thought was a weighty namesake for a girl from the trailer park."

"Ashleigh," I say.

"Ash-leigh. That feels like a weighty name, too. A mom who had hopes for her child."

You can be anything. She never thought I'd be a prostitute. "She'd be so disappointed."

"Maybe." Penny comes to sit down on the

other side of Ky. "Or maybe she'd be proud of you for surviving. It's a lot easier to give up when things get that hard."

"Or maybe she'd rather I died than become this."

"No. Never. No mother would want her child to die. Because that's the end. This way, there's more. It doesn't always feel like it, but there's more."

Ky seems so fragile on the bed. "More for him."

"So much more. A lifetime of hope and yearning and loving."

I glance at her. "I know who you are. Penny Scott. You own this place."

"With my husband, yes. The Den is our safe space. You'll find your own."

Something about the implication in her voice makes me look at her sharply. "It won't be with Sutton. We aren't... We aren't like that."

"Okay."

"I'm serious. He pays me for..." Tears spill over my cheeks. "He pays me for sex."

She doesn't look shocked. "He's downstairs right now. Been there for a few hours now. How much is he paying you for this time?"

I turn away. He's only downstairs out of guilt

right now. He only found me tonight out of guilt. *You're seventeen. How old did you think I am? Eighteen. At least.* "You don't understand."

Her footfalls cross the carpet. She places a hand on the crown of my head, soft and absolving. "No, I don't understand. I don't think many women do, but they'll judge you anyway, won't they? They'll think they know better, because it's easier than acknowledging the truth—that we're all vulnerable, that we're all one second away from a life of desperation. It isn't something you brought on yourself. It's something you're surviving, and you're doing it with more grace and more strength than those people could dream about."

Tears are falling freely now. "I don't know what to do about Ky. He's so young and so reckless. Sometimes I think he wants to die."

"If that's what he wants, you can't stop him."

"Can't I?" I turn pleading eyes to her, this woman who's a stranger, this person who's shown me more compassion than I could have imagined.

"No," she offers gently, "But you can sit with him. That's what you're doing, and it's a beautiful thing. Would you like to take a break? You can have something to eat? I'll wait with him."

"No, thank you," I say on a damp sigh.

Her expression is soft. "I'll have a tray sent up, then."

She's been gone a few minutes when Ky stirs on the bed. I'm at his side, offering a drink of water to his parched lips before he can speak. "What did I do?" he asks, his voice hoarse.

"You didn't do anything," I say, unable to stem the flow of tears. It's like a faucet that's been turned on—and the handle broke off. There's no way to make them stop now. "It was me. I was gone, and you were worried about me."

Even in this state the concern comes into his dark eyes. "Where were you?"

"There's this guy."

"Only sad stories start like that."

My heart squeezes. "I know."

"Don't get attached, Ash. You know that."

"I messed up," I whisper.

His eyelids droop heavy, and I know he's about to sleep again. I hold his hand so he'll know he's not alone. Even if he can't hear me, he'll know that much. "Not your fault," he mumbles, and I don't know whether he's talking about his bad trip or getting attached to Sutton. Maybe both.

✧   ✧   ✧

Sutton

I'M NURSING THE same glass of bourbon. It doesn't taste like anything. Hugo's here with me. If I had to guess, Damon Scott called him. He loves to pull our strings like we're puppets. He has a glass of water, because as soon as he's done, he has to drive home to his wife and baby.

"Get the hell out of here," I say, clenching my hands around the glass.

"There's no need to get hostile, mon ami. I'm not going anywhere."

Sometimes Hugo really is a bastard. "I don't need a babysitter."

"*Oui. Bon.* I'm not going to nurse you."

I swear he gets more French the more he wants to annoy me. "I'm not having some kind of weird rebound relationship because Harper and Christopher got married. I just got to know her, and I care about her as a friend, so I'm making sure she's okay."

There. That all sounded very reasonable.

Too bad it's a bunch of shit.

Hugo gives a French sigh and takes a sip of water.

The Den is pretty empty. It's a Wednesday night, but even so this is sparse. It's more than a bar. It's the playground of the rich and licentious.

It's also a modern-day salon for free thinkers. "Where the hell is everyone?"

"I think they took one look at your face and ran away scared."

I run a hand over my face and hair. "I'm not that bad."

"Well, I think Damon Scott may send you a bill for lost service."

Before I can respond, the door opens. Blue comes inside, bringing with him a wave of cold, damp air. It must have started raining. Now I'm very sure that someone called them. Hugo and Blue were two of my closest friends.

Along with Christopher.

The four of us met every week, no matter how busy we got with work. We're sounding boards and support. We're steady rocks in an upside-down world. We even had a name, being the ambitious bastards that we are. Thieves Club. Because every dollar earned is a dollar taken from someone else. Whether we earned that money through investments or buildings, or in Hugo's case, sleeping with wealthy women.

Blue sits down with that damned military bearing. "What did I miss?"

"Sutton's feeling very sad over *la courtisane.*"

My eyebrows go up. "You know what she

does."

"But of course. I recognize her from the street corner. Very pretty girl."

"Do you know how *old* she is?"

Hugo gives it a quick thought, as if doing a calculation. "I would say, seventeen."

"Damn."

"My knowledge of women is unrivaled."

"Then can you talk to her. She feels ashamed of what she's done to survive."

"Is she ashamed? Or are you?"

"Hell," I say on a growl. "I'm not ashamed of her. I'm goddamn pissed at everyone who made this her only choice. Her mother and father and whoever else made this happen."

"I don't think she wants to hear from an old colleague, but I'm always here if she needs me. There are some stains that never go away."

That makes me raise my eyebrows. Even Blue looks surprised. He's the one who speaks first. "You always seem so damn self-assured. I didn't think you minded."

"I don't mind the good nights, of which there were many. The bad nights tend to linger."

"I think she's had bad nights."

"You will help her through them more than I. Be patient. Be kind. Be loving."

The word is like a slap. "I don't love her."

Blue clears his throat, and I follow his blue gaze. Ashleigh stands there looking like a betrayed goddess, hurt and proud and unbearably dignified. *I don't love her.* The words echo in the air around us. There's nothing I can say to fix them, nothing that wouldn't sound false.

The door opens again, and I half expect to see Christopher. Which would be ridiculous as he's on his honeymoon. But he would complete the four of us. He would know what to do about Ashleigh. I need to stop fucking wanting him.

Instead it's a man I don't recognize, someone tall and lean, wearing a suit. He looks like any one of the men I'd pass in the high-rises around downtown.

Ashleigh's brown eyes widen. "You."

He gives her an empty, implacable stare. "And you are?"

"I'm Ky's friend. And you aren't going anywhere near him."

"Ah." The man doesn't look worried about her pronouncement. "So he is here."

"You don't really care about him. You only want him for sex. You have more money than you know what to do with, but you don't love him. You can't love him." Her lower lip trembles. "You refuse to love him."

The man looks back at her gravely. "I never claimed to love him, but I can take care of him. A good deal better than you, I'm willing to bet."

"I don't care," Ashleigh says. "You're Mr. Monopoly, made of paper and plastic. You're not real. You don't get to visit him once a month and then come here and pretend to care."

"Ash." The word comes soft and weak from the top of the stairs. It's the boy. Ky. He looked young when I found him barely breathing. He looks even younger now, clinging to the post. In a few seconds the man—Mr. Monopoly—has climbed the steps and captured Ky in his arms. "Shhhh," he murmurs. "I've got you."

"You're not taking him," Ashleigh warns, looking ready to fight him off physically.

"Ashleigh," Ky says, reaching for her with a weak arm. Ashleigh clasps his hand in hers. "Let me… go with him. Let me… go."

She looks sick, like she might throw up. I want to take her in my arms, but I can't. I can't forget that she's seventeen. I can't forget the sins I've already committed. If she wants to fight this asshole, I'll do it for her. But she takes a step back. "Don't," she whispers. "Don't get attached."

"You too." An uneven laugh. "You too, Ash."

The man gathers Ky in a secure hold and strides out. There are a driver and Bentley waiting outside. Mr. Monopoly isn't so wrong of a name. It makes me wonder what he's doing strolling the streets for his lovers. I suppose people could ask the same of me. As if they're some lower class, some undeserving group of people. They don't need love, right? Not when I'm paying them.

You have more money than you know what to do with, but you don't love him. You can't love him. You refuse to love him.

She wasn't only talking to him. She was talking about me.

Chapter Twenty-Two

Ashleigh

Sutton takes me home and brings me inside. I'm too exhausted to protest. It's the kind of exhaustion that hollows me out.

Sutton puts me in the shower and washes my hair. Then he puts me in an armchair clad only in one of his white T-shirts. He brings me a steaming cup of tea, but I can't drink anything. I'm tired but plagued by an agitation that makes it impossible to rest.

He stands in front of me. "Tell me where you're from."

"No."

"You don't have family that could help you?"

"I told you. My secrets are my own."

"Not if you're in danger on the streets. If nothing else, Ky proved that much. I care about you."

"The way Mr. Monopoly cares?"

"Yes, damn it. Is that so wrong? Why can we pay money but not give a damn?"

"I don't owe you this. You didn't buy my secrets."

"I bought your time," he says, as if cataloging a purchase order. "I bought your body. Your kisses. Is that right? Only those things?"

"Yes." And my love. I gave that to him for free, though he doesn't know. It would probably horrify him to know that I feel that way. Maybe he'd run away then. Except I can't bring myself to tell him. It would strip me naked in a way I haven't been.

"Then let me buy your secrets."

"What?"

"How much are they? Name your price."

I stare at him. "My secrets aren't for sale."

"Everything is for sale."

God. Maybe this is the problem with being rich. You feel entitled to everything. I give him a ridiculous amount. "One hundred thousand dollars."

"Done." He walks over to a desk and pulls out something—a small leather rectangle that looks like a checkbook. A pen. He scribbles something down. Then he walks over to me and hands me the check. *One hundred thousand dollars.*

"This is ridiculous," I say, but I sound more panicked than doubtful. "This isn't real."

"It's real enough. Needs a last name, though. You ready to tell me that?"

With my last name he could probably find out everything else. That's another one of those rich people things. "I broke my mom's favorite vase when I was eight. I was so afraid of telling her, and seeing her disappointed, that I buried all the pieces in the backyard. One day it just vanished and she never knew where it went."

"That's not a real secret."

"You didn't specify the kind of secret you were buying."

"My daddy used to hit me so hard my feet would come off the ground. I would try not to make a sound. I felt like that was how I'd win, by not making a sound. Now that I'm a grown-up I think, why didn't I scream? Why didn't I tell? Why didn't I tell him he was a mean bastard?"

"I'm sorry."

"I didn't want to fall in love with anyone. Then I met Christopher and discovered I'm bisexual. He wasn't. So I had to love him as a business partner. Then there was Harper." He gives a soft laugh. "You'd think I would learn."

"Don't," I whisper.

"Don't get attached? It's too late for that, Ashleigh. Love is the great human experiment. We try it again and again. It doesn't matter how many times we fail or how much it hurts."

"It always hurts."

"I have this theory that sometimes it doesn't. If that person loves you back."

"My daddy never hit me."

Sutton goes still, knowing this is the real secret. "Ash," he says, the way Ky says.

"He never seemed to care much about me. I thought it was just—the way he loved me. That distant father kind of thing. More busy with work than his family. And then I turned fifteen. I needed to get bras—real bras, not training bras. And he started…"

"I love you," Sutton says, in this fierce way. It feels like swords and drawbridges, those words. Like he wants to go to battle for me. And when he says that, it doesn't hurt.

"He'd come up behind me. Always behind me. Never facing me. He'd reach around and touch me, and I'd go very still, because I was afraid. Why was I afraid? Why didn't I scream or yell or call him a mean bastard?"

"Because he's your father," Sutton says gently. "Parents have that power."

"He touched me under my shirt. Under my bra."

"Christ."

"I think I could have stayed living there, if it was that. That's the worst part. I told my mother." A hollow forms in my chest. "She didn't believe me. She said I was lying, that if I wanted to say that, then I should just leave, because she didn't want to see me."

"So you left."

"It hurt so much," I tell him, tears slick on my cheeks. "She was my mother. My everything. Every day she'd say, *I love you.* But what did it mean? Nothing."

He holds me until the sobbing stops. I turn in his arms, press a kiss to his neck. He becomes very still, and I squirm, trying to get closer.

"Let's go to bed," he says gently, and that sounds fine to me.

He lifts me in his arms and carries me there. The sheets are cool on my legs. He pulls the covers up to me. I watch as he pulls off his clothes, leaving him in only boxer briefs.

I curl into his arms, and he gathers me close.

And then does nothing.

My leg presses over his, and I can feel his arousal, but he only lies there holding me. I run my hand along his broad chest. My lips find his shoulder, his jaw, his neck.

"Ashleigh."

"What?" I whisper. "I'm not tired."

"You're exhausted, but that's not the point."

"Then what's the point?"

"I can't do that with you," he finally says, sounding resigned. And very serious.

"What?" I scramble up to stare at him. "Why?"

"Because you're seventeen."

"I was seventeen before when we did that."

"Yes. And that's something I have to face, something I should have faced before I touched you. Maybe part of me knew, but didn't want to think about it. It doesn't matter, because I know now. And I want you more than life, but I can't have you."

"I *want* to have sex with you."

He groans. "Ashleigh. I can't do that and still respect myself."

Hurt courses through me, followed closely by anger. The anger feels safer. "This isn't fair. I've been on my own for six months. I'm more of a grown-up than some kid in college where his parents pay for everything."

"Yes."

"And I've had sex before. Bad sex. Good sex."

"Yes."

"But you're still not going to have sex with me? That's bullshit, Sutton. I know you're trying to do the right thing, but all you're doing is taking away any power I might have had. This is my decision."

"Hell, Ashleigh. You're right about every fucking thing, but I still can't touch you. I've become too much like my father but it stops now. You made me strong enough to stop. If you can live the life you've had, if you can survive it, then I can get over the goddamn heartbreak. I'm not going to touch you without understanding the consequences. Not anymore."

"What consequences?"

"That you care about me," he says gently.

I look away, but not before he sees the tears in my eyes. "I don't."

"And that I care about you. Come here and let me hold you. Let me have that much."

I want to tell him no out of spite. The irony doesn't escape me, that weeks ago I wouldn't have wanted him to touch me, wouldn't have wanted any man to touch me. And now I'm mad at Sutton that he won't have sex with me. "Why is caring about me so wrong?"

"It's not. God, Ashleigh. It's not wrong to care, but that's going to make it hurt so much more when we can't be together. You're seventeen. You have a whole life ahead of you. I'm thirty-two, and I have no business tying you to me right now, when you're vulnerable."

"I'm not vulnerable," I say, but that's so clearly a lie that I laugh softly. It's a watery laugh. I've been sobbing and laughing so much that I feel a little unhinged.

He gathers me close to him, his arms tight, his lips on my temple soft. "Do you know how much it hurts not to take you right now? But it's right. It should hurt. That's love."

✧   ✧   ✧

ASHLEIGH

IN THE MORNING I wake up in bed alone. Sunlight streams through the window, drawing lines across the rumpled white sheets. Outside Bowie crows that it's time to wake up. It's a peaceful place to sleep, a home that isn't mine. Or is it? Maybe Ky can live with Mr. Monopoly and I can live with Sutton. And maybe fairy tales come true.

I find Sutton at the kitchen table waiting for

me. I recognize the check from last night. Dread forms in my stomach. No, I can't expect anything. There is no happy ending for a prostitute who works on the street. Only tragedies for us.

He hands me a slip of paper. *Adeleide Johnson*, it says in bold block letters. Along with an address. "My investigator found that this morning."

My heart clenches.

"Mom," I whisper.

"It looks like she left him when you ran away."

She left him? That should make me feel better. I'm not sure if I can forgive her for not being there when I need her. I'm not sure I have a choice. The heart moves without permission. Before I've even decided one way or the other, I've forgiven her.

I also know things can never go back to the way they were. After living on the streets, I can never go back to being a girl. Something broke when she turned away from me, some thread from mother to daughter. Even if I see her, and I want to, my breath catches with how much I want to, it won't ever be the same.

Sutton pushes the check forward, and I see that it's not the same one from last night. It has a much bigger number on it. An additional zero, for one thing. I stare at it, uncomprehending. "What is that?"

He meets my eyes with somber determination. "I can't be with you. Not like this. Part of me will always wonder if you chose me because there aren't other choices."

"Sutton."

"Maybe it does take away your power. God knows you've earned that much. But I love you too much to take the chance. If I took advantage of you now, I couldn't live with myself."

The realization makes me ache. "So what are you saying? Goodbye?"

He looks down at his hands, where they're clasped between his knees. He's masculine strength and contemplation. "Did you know I thought it was my fault? That Harper chose Christopher? That my love wasn't as deep as his. That I was shallower, and she could sense that about me. That I was weaker because I loved two people instead of one."

"Sutton, no."

"Yes." His voice turns hoarse. "The thing is, I was right. It was a shallower love than I was capable of, and maybe she *did* see it. It wasn't diminished because there were two of them. It was diminished because I was waiting for you."

I shake my head, unseeing. "Then why are you sending me away?"

"I loved them with a selfish, shallow love. I wanted them for myself. But you... God, Ashleigh. I love you the real way. The deep way. The way where I need you to be safe and secure and strong more than I need to breathe. So yes. Yes. This is goodbye."

"That's not fair." Even as I say the words I know they make me sound my age. Like the seventeen-year-old he's afraid to take advantage of. Maybe that's what I am. I'm innocent and world-weary. I'm young and ineffably tired at the same time. I'm everything. Why can't I be everything? Whoever decided we had to be only one thing—the virgin or the whore?

He taps the check. "There's enough here for college. For medical school. Or to travel the world. Do what you want, build a life for yourself."

I hold back tears. "Two roads diverged in a wood, and I—I took the one less traveled by."

"And that has made all the difference."

My lip trembles. "I can't believe you're doing this."

He sounds faintly wry. "Me either, honestly."

"So you want me to go date guys? Marry them?"

"If that's what you want," he says hoarsely. "But if—"

"If."

"If you build a life, and there's room for me in it, I'll be there."

THE FUNNY THING about holding a check for two million dollars is that you can't actually cash it without some form of identification. It's Blue himself—with those familiar blue eyes I would recognize from anywhere, so like Sutton's—who drives me away from the ranch in his black Expedition.

He looks casually competent and intimidating across the large dash. "Blue Security will manage your lodgings and care until such time as you take possession of the funds."

"Is that your way of saying I'm not homeless anymore?"

He gives me an appreciative look. "So you're the straightforward type of client."

"I don't think I'm a client at all because I'm not paying you. But yeah, I think I'd prefer things straightforward. I've had enough of being in the dark."

"I assume you don't have ID. We can get a rush application for your birth certificate and social security card. From there we can get you a state ID card."

I look out the window, at the farmland that's rapidly turning into city. We're leaving Sutton. We're leaving Haven. We're leaving the darkest evening of the year, and there should be some comfort in that. It would feel better if it didn't feel like my heart stayed behind. "My mother might have those things."

"You don't have to see her."

Which answers the question about how much Sutton told him. "It would be quicker. And the sooner you can stop babysitting me on Sutton's dime, the better. Besides, I want to see her."

"You're the boss," he says in a tone which means the opposite.

I slide the piece of paper with her address over. "I'd like to go here."

We don't stop at some waystation, some beige motel where I can be transferred to someone less senior. Instead Blue punches the address into the GPS, and we take a drive into one of the sadder suburbs of Tanglewood. The cardboard McMansions have fallen into disrepair. Apartment buildings have sprung up where there used to be parks. It's in one of those tired-looking apartment buildings that we stop.

There's a crush of air as a bus stops down the street. Someone steps off the bus, looking thinner than I remember, older than I remember. It's her. I'm frozen to the ground. All I feel is love and hurt. It's a struggle to hold on to any anger.

She has her head down as she walks towards us. When she gets close she looks up. A gasp that can be heard across the parking lot. Her groceries fall to the gravel. A peach rolls through a puddle. Then she's running to me, catching me in her arms. "My girl. My sweet girl. You're alive."

She hugs me, and I cry. Part of me wants to go back to the way everything might have been— if she had left with me when I first told her, if I could trust her. I would live in this sad little apartment, and I would have been happy like this. It would have been home.

Instead I give her Blue's card. "I'm here." My words stutter and choke out of me. "I wanted you to know that—that I'm safe now. You can call me here."

And then I get in the passenger seat of the car and close the door.

Blue murmurs something to her, and slowly,

aching, she moves to the sidewalk. He gathers up her groceries—all except the peach, which is ruined now—and gives them to her in the bags. I love her as a mother. I always will. But that love has a deep, indelible crack running through it. I want to have her in my life. But I can't ask her for anything.

Not even my own birth certificate.

Blue backs out of the space and drives me away.

CHAPTER TWENTY-THREE

SUTTON

I T WOULD BE so easy to look her up. So easy to find out where she is, to show up where she lives. It's the greatest struggle of my day, not searching for her. I scan every face when I walk into a restaurant or a coffee shop.

I look for her in the street, but I don't let myself look her up.

My grief this time looks different. It's not about drinking or feeling sorry for myself. I throw myself into work, building my own life. Building something I can be proud of.

Something that would make me worthy of her.

I'm sitting in my office, working on the plans when someone knocks.

"I'm eating," I tell Mrs. Ness without looking up. There's a turkey sandwich, potato salad, and a large slice of key lime pie waiting for me on my desk.

"I'm not Mrs. Ness," comes a voice from my memory.

I look up, and there's Christopher. He looks exactly like I remember him: handsome and diffident. Other people see him as distant, but I've always known that he's shy. "Hello."

"Can I come in?" He lifts up a white paper bag. "I brought gifts."

"Contraband. Excellent."

Benny's is a BBQ place down the street from our office. Rather, down the street from our office when we had one. The short-lived, ill-fated company of Bardot and Mayfair.

He hands over the bag, and I look inside to find two Styrofoam containers filled to the brim. I pass one back to him and keep one to myself. Neither of us bother with plastic silverware.

I take a bite and close my eyes on a moan. "God, yes."

Christopher does the same, and the expression he makes is pure erotic pleasure, even with the hint of barbecue sauce on the corner of his mouth. The sight arrests me for a moment. Probably the sight of a beautiful man always will, but it's a faraway kind of appreciation.

I take another bite of the warm meat. "Do

you know how long it's been?"

"Probably since you left."

"Mrs. Ness would never order from there."

"Pussy," he says, though the word holds no heat.

Both of us took instructions from the older woman. She was our office manager when we shared an office. When we split up, somehow I ended up with her, which I was grateful for. I suppose it was compensation for Christopher getting Harper.

When I've finished the full line of ribs I move on to the jalapeno bread. "So what is this? A peace offering? Or do you need me to sign some papers?"

"Hell," he says. "Why not both?"

I have to laugh at that. "You're more of a bastard than me, Christopher."

He looks affronted. "Of course I am. What, you think stomping around for a few weeks makes up for a lifetime of being a cold and conniving bastard?"

"You're not as bad as everything thinks you are."

"I'm not as good as you thought I was, either."

"No, probably not. Nobody can live up to the

pedestals they're put on, can they?"

"Here's the thing about me and Harper. You loved her for everything good about her. You loved her in spite of her flaws, but I love her because of them. She's vain and selfish and wicked."

"She's not—"

"Yes, she is. She's also talented and generous and so damn caring it makes my teeth hurt. She's a whole person, the good and the bad, and I love every single part of it. She deserves someone who loves every part of her. And you deserve someone who loves every part of you."

"Hey," I say. "What's not to love? A deadbeat alcoholic with anger management issues."

"There will be someone who loves that part about you."

Maybe I already had that person. Maybe I gave her up.

And I understand what he means.

The fact that she lived on the street. The fact that she prostituted herself. There are men who would judge her for that. They might be with her despite that, but they wouldn't appreciate her because of that. When I look at her time on the corner, I see only her strength. Her survival. The world would be such a dimmer place if she were gone. It tried to put out her light. Her father. Even her mother, for all that she repented later.

Maybe Christopher had a point. I saw Harper's flaws, but he sees them as strengths.

The same way I see Ashleigh. That's love.

✧　✧　✧

ASHLEIGH

SUGAR DIPS HER paw into my teacup and drinks. Then she walks across my organic chemistry homework, leaving wet prints. A stack sits precariously at the edge of my desk, organized by a system of deadlines, subjects, and random thoughts in my head.

There's a knock on my dorm room door.

It's Jason from my class. "Did you get notes from political science?"

"Yeah, do you want to see them?" When he nods I pull out a sheaf of papers.

He whistles. "This is a lot."

"Professor Morris was on a roll."

"Can I make copies of this and return them?"

"Sure."

He pauses at my door, and Sugar eyes his ankles like she wants to attack. It's a private dorm, so we're allowed to have an animal if we pay an enormous fee. But it means no more mice hunting. Instead Sugar likes to attack my friends' feet. "Maybe I could drop them back tonight. Would you like to go out for dinner?"

A date. He's asking me on a date. He isn't the first boy to do so, but he's the first one where I've thought about saying yes. Jason is cute, and he's kind. I think about Sutton, but he's not here. He left. Part of me wants to be pissed, but part of me also knows he was right. I have to at least date another boy in my lifetime. That has to be part of the experiment. *If you build a life, and there's room for me in it, I'll be there.* "Yes," I say. "Dinner would be great."

Chapter Twenty-Four

Five years later

"**A**SHLEIGH JOHNSON."

Until the moment my name is called, part of me doesn't believe it's real. I stand up and climb the steps to the stage. The band plays their short crossing-the-stage montage. It's a small department in a small school, with a graduating class of 20 in the School of Natural Science. The dean smiles at me and mispronounced my name—*Ash-lee*—and hands me a rolled sheet of paper. We pose for pictures. It feels like a blur, like maybe this is a dream instead of real.

Only when I'm crossing the other side do I see him.

The audience sits on white folding chairs across the green lawn, the mass of them moving. Parents. Siblings. Friends. That's why he stands out. Other people look down and leaf through the program. Other people wave at their children waiting for their turn. Other people are on their phones.

My mother wipes tears from her eyes.

Even Ky has his camera in front of his face, snapping photos.

Sutton is completely still, watching me in a suit, a solid point in a storm. I would recognize those blue eyes from outer space. That wild mane of hair and square jaw. That body that looks as comfortable in jeans and a T-shirt as he does in a custom suit.

The rest of the ceremony takes forever.

Then we throw our hats into the air. Even before they've hit the ground, I'm pushing through the crowd, searching for him. He finds me and pulls me into a bear hug. He smells like sunshine and male spice. I almost remembered this scent in my dreams.

"Congratulations," he says to my ear.

There's a crowd of people around us. This isn't a private moment, except it is. We're the solid place in the middle of a storm. "You got my invitation."

"I was coming either way. It was better not to sneak in, though."

That makes me laugh. The security on this private university campus is laughable. Then my smile fades. "I wasn't sure you'd come. Or that you'd remember."

"Every day. Every night. Every goddamn hour."

"It wasn't so long that the two of us were together. Not compared to a lifetime."

"A lifetime wouldn't be worth much without love."

I hold my breath. "Love?"

He presses his face into my hair and breathes deep. "I have this theory."

"It doesn't matter how many times we fail or how much it hurts."

"It doesn't matter how long we have to wait."

It feels almost impossible that he could have come. That he would love me and I would love him. One chance in a billion. The great human experiment. "Did it work?"

Blue eyes search mine. "Let's find out."

That makes me laugh, though I'm not sure why. It's a joyous sound.

Sutton pulls something from his pocket and drops to one knee. A brilliant cushion cut diamond sparkles at me from a blue Tiffany box. "Marry me."

Emotion tightens my throat. Tears prick my eyes. People turn to watch us. There's clapping and cheering. We're surrounded by friends and by strangers. All of them understand what's happening, because this is more than an experiment.

It's the great human constant. "Yes."

The people around us go wild. More hats fly into the air.

Sutton pulls me into his arms and kisses me like he's never letting go.

✧ ✧ ✧

ASHLEIGH

I TAKE HIM back to my dorm room, which is swarming with students heading to after-parties and a few families helping their graduates move out. Sugar hisses when she sees Sutton and runs out of the room. "Don't take it personally," I say. "She hates men. And my neighbor keeps cat treats on his nightstand."

He gets this look on his face like he's holding something in. A comment. A question.

"What?" I ask, pausing in the act of moving a box of books from my bed.

It's like the question is pulled forcibly from his body, catching on everything on the way out. "Have there been a lot of men here? Christ. I wasn't supposed to ask that."

I try to look stern. "Are you slut shaming

me?"

"God. No. I'm a caveman. There's no excuse for it."

He's so adorable when he's flustered. Adorable and handsome and yes—there's something distinctly caveman about him. The suit and slacks can't disguise the primal male who's come to claim his mate. "Have there been a lot of women for you?"

"No."

"What about men?"

"No, but I am friends with Christopher again. Just friends. There hasn't been anyone for me. I have five years' worth of frustration built up. Five years of hitting the gym and cold showers. Five years of beating off to the image of you in my bed. You aren't going to keep me waiting, are you, Ashleigh?"

Once I've cleared space on the bed I drift toward him, wrapping my arms around his neck. We're inches away. "I dated," I murmur.

His hands tighten on me. "I'm not mad at you. I swear. It's just that I need to go run ten miles, and then we can have this conversation."

I laugh softly. "I never brought them back here."

He doesn't relax. "You have a right to date

whoever you want."

"Or went to their place."

"It's natural to want to explore."

"There hasn't been anyone I wanted except you."

"Thank fuck," he says, pressing his lips to mine. His tongue searches into my mouth, finding my tongue, my teeth, the silk on the insides of my cheeks. It's like he wants to explore every square centimeter of me, like he wants to breathe me into his lungs.

We fall in a tangle of limbs on my twin-sized bed, fully clothed, our lips together. His legs are too long for the space, and we bump into the headboard and my nightstand.

"Sorry," I say, gasping as my elbow hits the wall.

"Is there room in your life for me?" he asks, his blue eyes deep.

There's a lot I don't know about my life. I graduated with honors with a bachelor's in biology. I have acceptance into medical school. There will be long hours and interning and a ridiculous amount of work to achieve my dreams. But I know one thing. There's room for love.

"Yes," I say stroking his wild curls back from his forehead. There are new lines on his face.

Stress lines. Grooves on the side of his mouth. This isn't a man afraid of hard work.

"I love you, Sutton Mayfair."

"Good," he says, turning me onto my back. "Because I've waited long enough."

CHAPTER TWENTY-FIVE

THE CAR PASSES the Den and I tense in the passenger seat.

"You okay?" he murmurs. Of course he sees the anxiety building even though I've tried to hide it. He told me we were coming to the west side. I knew it would raise some memories.

"Sure," I lie.

He mutters a quiet curse. "It's too soon. We can come back another time."

"No." I'm insistent. "I want to see my surprise."

His hand runs over his face and through his hair in that way he has when he's frustrated at himself. It makes him look rumpled and sexy. "I should have gotten you flowers as a surprise. Balloons. Chocolate. Do you like chocolate?"

"We'll get chocolate later."

We only have a few weeks until I start medical school this fall, so we're making the most of it— riding horses around the ranch, leaving for local fairs and cultural festivals. It's like we're both determined to make up for all the time we waited to be together.

This morning he woke me up with something new: a surprise.

Knowing Sutton, it could literally be anything.

We pull to a stop on my regular street corner, and my pulse speeds up. How many nights did I stand on that corner, hugging the lamppost, trying to gather the nerve to get a customer? I'd have thought the years would make it easier, but shame sinks in my stomach.

He mutters another curse.

I stare at the two square yards of concrete. I can already see every crack in my mind. Every uneven place in the bricks of the building. Every rut in the street. This place is more familiar to me than anything I know now—my dorm room, the university. No matter how much time has passed, this corner's emblazoned in my mind.

I'm trembling by the time Sutton opens my car door.

He pulls me to standing. "Should we get out of here?"

"No," I say stubbornly. "Not until I get my surprise."

His blue eyes are tender. "You know I love

you."

"You know I love you, too."

He pulls me forward and then steps out of the way, revealing the sugar factory. I have every inch of that place mapped out as well, the window I hopped through, the fire escape I climbed. I could sketch the inside as quickly as I can sketch the human heart.

Except none of it's there anymore.

The building has been restored, the exterior fixed and the brick lightened. Yellow light presses against the windows. Smoke curls from somewhere at the top of the building. A sign over the front door reads, *Safe Haven*.

As if in a trance I move toward the entrance, Sutton following behind.

A plaque marks the front entrance, with the following verse:

The woods are lovely, dark, and deep,
But I have promises to keep.

I take a shuddering breath to fortify miles. I have miles to go before I sleep.

The door has a very serious-looking lock on it, with a note. *This is a home for women, LGBTQ, and at-risk populations. You are safe here.* A little lower, it continues, *Many of our guests are victims of sexual assault, domestic violence, human trafficking, and other trauma. Visitors must be approved by the administration and submit to a background check.*

And at the end, *This premises is protected by Blue Security.*

I look back at Sutton—shocked, honored, overwhelmed. "You did this?"

"I had to do something. You were going to be a doctor and save the world. I figured I could be responsible for saving this corner. You were my first guest."

"Ky was," I say, my eyes wet with tears.

"Ky helped me," he admits. "Along with Hannah, Blue's wife. A lot of people pitched in. Mostly what I did was knock down walls and then rebuild them."

"I can't believe he knew about it and didn't tell me."

"He was sworn to secrecy. And he said if you knew about it, you'd insist on helping. I couldn't have seen you without needing you. It was bad enough knowing you were somewhere in the city, and that if I only looked you up, only called, I could have found you."

I run to him and throw my arms around him. He catches me in a secure grip, twirling me around on this street corner. It used to mean sadness and pain, being here. Hunger. And that persistent cold of winter that never really goes away. Now it's a place of hope.

"I love you," I say. "Love you, love you, love you."

I press mad kisses across his eyebrows, his cheeks, his chin. I feel a little wild with how much I love this man, but he returns the sentiment without missing a beat, pressing me against the wall, breathing me in, and kissing my neck, biting gently and then soothing with his tongue.

A car passes by on the street and honks. I jump apart from him like a guilty teenager. He pulls back more slowly, his blue eyes laughing. "If I had known you'd react like this, I'd have brought you here a long time ago?"

"You built me a castle in the sky." I rest my head on his chest, feeling the safety and surety of his arms. The truth is I was safe from the moment he first kissed me against the wall, even if I didn't know it. That's Sutton. Kind and generous. And loving.

My hand rests on his shoulder, the sapphires sparkling around the diamond.

"You were never for sale, you know that, right?" he murmurs in my ear.

"I know," I murmur. "I was just waiting for you."

Epilogue

Sutton

I WONDERED WHY unconventional, defiant Harper had wanted a wedding in a grand church. What I didn't understand is that when you get married, you want the weight of thousands of years of tradition to protect your love. The commitment, that comes from inside you. It's the rest of the world that bears witness.

Our wedding happens in the holiest place I know of—on the wide-open tract of land with my name on the deed. My name, along with Ashleigh's name. Two hundred acres are more than our home. They're our domain. I'm the king of this earth, these trees, that sky. And she's my queen. Small, as kingdoms go—but big enough to build a lifetime together.

Christopher comes to stand beside me. "Mrs. Cheung would lose her shit."

I have my foot on the fence, arm slung over

the wood. The rough grain probably mars the silk and the wool, but I can't be bothered to move. "Good thing she's not here."

"You nervous?"

The same question I asked him. The same answer. "No."

"You haven't known her that long."

A smile curves my lips. Harper has really changed Christopher. Or maybe it's the twins. Either way the man I knew five years ago wouldn't have made a joke. "I've waited too damn long already."

I glance back at the house. White curtains ruffle against the window. I'm not the one having doubts, but maybe she is. She's still young, after all. There's medical school and then residency. And then an entire lifetime. Maybe she doesn't want a washed-up cowboy for a husband.

"She's coming," Christopher says, reading my damn mind.

"I'm going to check on her."

He puts a hand on my arm. "Give her time."

I glare at him. "You're making me wait because Harper asked for me."

Before their wedding, Harper wanted to talk to me, to make sure I was okay with their marriage. I wasn't really, not at the time. Now I see that they're right for each other. What kind of bastard gets in the way of true love? Christopher gives me a slight smile. "Maybe I should go check on her."

And see her in her wedding dress? "No."

"Turnabout's fair play."

"Absolutely not."

He puts a hand to his heart in mock injury. "You don't trust me?"

"Not as far as I can throw you or your hotels."

"Of course you should marry him," he says in a pretend-stern voice. "He's nice and rich and good with dogs and children. It's too bad he's shit at poker."

"Fuck you." I land a solid punch to his arm, and he recoils, scowling. That's about how well I play poker: terribly. I can fight or play or work, but I can't bluff worth a damn.

"I suppose now's a good time to bring up that contract."

I slide him a sideways glance. "Told you my terms."

"And I gave you a counteroffer."

"You forgot how shitty I am at poker. Take it or leave it."

"I didn't forget." He leans on the gate in a parallel position. "That's why there's a signed contract sitting on your desk, waiting for when you're back from your honeymoon."

I glance at him sharply. We were business partners once. Before we became lovers and then enemies. For the past five years we've been friends. This would be a change, but a welcome one. I hated that wedge between us. "Thank you."

"You should thank me. That was a damn hard bargain you drove."

"Some games you don't have to bluff to win."

"Is that Southern boy wisdom?" he says with a sardonic tone.

I narrow my eyes and glance at my watch. It's twenty minutes past the start time of the wedding. "Have you been distracting me? On fucking purpose?"

"Don't look so nervous. She's coming."

Twenty minutes late to her own wedding. I look at the open window again, where a white curtain waves gently in the wind. Does she need my help? Is she having second thoughts? It's not a small thing, marriage. I should give her all the time in the world, but I'm too impatient for that. I want her to be mine, before God, beneath the open sky, on this land that we own.

I want her right goddamn now.

✧ ✧ ✧

ASHLEIGH

I CAN'T WAIT.

I've been awake since 5 a.m., a bundle of excitement, counting down the hours until I could get married to the man I love. I'm already in my white undergarments—a corset, along with stockings and a garter belt. The summer air is too sticky to put on my dress until the moment I go downstairs. There's a textbook open on the desk where I've been attempting to pass the time.

A quick knock on the door, and Ky peeks his head in. I gasp and cover myself with the heavy book. "Give a girl some warning here."

He grins and strolls into the room.

"You don't have the parts I'm interested in, but if I were straight, I'd be all over that. You look like a goddamn cake."

I slap him on the arm. "Gee, thanks."

Penny follows him inside, holding a black velvet box. "Something for the bride. I heard you needed something blue, so I had this made for you."

A blush covers my cheeks. "Ky was supposed to get a ribbon or something."

"Close," Ky says, nudging me toward the box.

It feels strange to be standing in a room with two fully clothed people, but there's a lot about

SKYE WARREN

being a bride that's strange. I think this whole day will feel surreal. It definitely feels surreal as I open the box to reveal a sparkling garter belt. Thick plush lace serves as the base for an elaborate construction of diamonds and sapphires. "Oh my God," I breathe. "I can't—I can't wear this. Or accept it. This is too much."

Penny and Ky exchange a look as if my response doesn't surprise them. Penny and I have become close over the past few years, exchanging long emails. Which means I know her well enough to know that these aren't fake gems. This will be the real thing.

"It must be worth a fortune," I say with dismay.

"It's my gift to you," Penny says gently.

I make a face. "So there's nothing in that giant pile of white and silver presents from you?"

"It's not my *only* gift to you," she says. "But you're my good friend. If there's one day a girl deserves to be spoiled, it's her wedding day."

Tears prick my eyes, and I blink them back. "I don't deserve to be spoiled."

A palm on the middle of my back. Ky. A soft touch to the back of my hand. Penny. Friends when I thought I'd spend the rest of my short life alone. Some days I can take everything in stride—

graduating from college, living on the ranch. Even signing the deed with Sutton and his lawyer didn't make me lose it. But this... this garter. This ridiculous, over-the-top, incredible garter will be the death of me. A sob breaks free, and I know I'll ruin my makeup. It's too late. The sorrow and the guilt and the shame wrap around me. No matter how much I distract myself, they never truly leave. "Oh God," I say, gasping for breath. "I'm sorry, I'm sorry, I'm sorry."

"No, I'm sorry." Penny wraps me in a tight hug. "I feel awful. I thought it would be—no, it doesn't matter what I thought. It was a mistake. I'll take it back."

"You can't have it back," I say on a watery laugh. "It's mine now."

She gives a relieved smile. "There's my girl."

"Actually," Ky says from behind me. "Sutton will have to take it off in front of everyone and throw it to someone. I'm planning on catching it, so I'd appreciate a nice underhand in my direction."

Streaks of mascara line my hands. "Ugh, I must look terrible."

Penny guides me to the chair. "You look absolutely beautiful, but unless I want Sutton to go full protective caveman, we're going to have to wipe away the evidence of these tears."

She goes to work wiping off my old makeup while Ky puts the garter belt on me. "I'm sorry I freaked out," I say, feeling sheepish now that I have my emotions under control. "I guess I'm a little on edge today."

"Of course you are," Penny says.

Ky sighs. "It's hard to let go of the past shit. It rears its ugly head whenever I least expect it, which means of course it would show up for you today. I'm like hey, look, I'm happy. Then the past is like, remember this super depressing thing?"

There's a clench in my stomach, the place that always turns into a knot when I think of those years ago. My therapist says it's better to let the feelings run through me than shove them down deep. I'm still working on that. "I'm just grateful I have both of you to help me through it."

"And that you have Ky to do your makeup. No one does cat eyeliner like me."

I glance at the clock, worried. "I'm going to be late for my own wedding."

"You can't be late for your own wedding," Penny says prosaically. "What are they going to do? You're the bride. It starts whenever you walk in."

Thank you so much for reading MATING THEORY.

There are also many characters in this book who have their own story!

- Christopher and Harper. Read SURVIVAL OF THE RICHEST >
- Hugo and Bea. Read ESCORT now >
- Blue and Hannah. Read BETTER WHEN IT HURTS >
- Anders (the doctor)'s book. Read THE BISHOP >
- Damon and Penny, who own the Den. Read THE KING >

And don't miss the sexy virgin auction romance THE PAWN with Gabriel and Avery set in Tanglewood. *There's one way to save our house, one thing I have left of value—my body.*

"Wickedly brilliant, dark and addictive!"

– Jodi Ellen Malpas, #1 New York Times bestselling author

The price of survival...

Gabriel Miller swept into my life like a storm. He tore down my father with cold retribution, leaving him penniless in a hospital bed. I quit my private all-girl's college to take care of the only family I have left.

There's one way to save our house, one thing I have left of value.

My body.

A forbidden auction…

Gabriel appears at every turn. He seems to take pleasure in watching me fall. Other times he's the only kindness in a brutal underworld.

Except he's playing a deeper game than I know. Every move brings us together, every secret rips us apart. And when the final piece is played, only one of us can be left standing.

Excerpt from The Pawn

WIND WHIPS AROUND my ankles, flapping the bottom of my black trench coat. Beads of moisture form on my eyelashes. In the short walk from the cab to the stoop, my skin has slicked with humidity left by the rain.

Carved vines and ivy leaves decorate the ornate wooden door.

I have some knowledge of antique pieces, but I can't imagine the price tag on this one—especially exposed to the elements and the whims of vandals. I suppose even criminals know enough to leave the Den alone.

Officially the Den is a gentlemen's club, the old-world kind with cigars and private invitations. Unofficially it's a collection of the most powerful men in Tanglewood. Dangerous men. Criminals, even if they wear a suit while breaking the law.

A heavy brass knocker in the shape of a fierce lion warns away any visitors. I'm desperate enough to ignore that warning. My heart thuds in my chest and expands out, pulsing in my fingers, my toes. Blood rushes through my ears, drowning out the whoosh of traffic behind me.

I grasp the thick ring and knock—once, twice.

Part of me fears what will happen to me behind that door. A bigger part of me is afraid the door won't open at all. I can't see any cameras set into the concrete enclave, but they have to be watching. Will they recognize me? I'm not sure it would help if they did. Probably best that they see only a desperate girl, because that's all I am now.

The softest scrape comes from the door. Then it opens.

I'm struck by his eyes, a deep amber color—like expensive brandy and almost translucent. My breath catches in my throat, lips frozen against words like *please* and *help.* Instinctively I know they won't work; this isn't a man given to mercy. The tailored cut of his shirt, its sleeves carelessly rolled up, tells me he'll extract a price. One I can't afford to pay.

There should have been a servant, I thought. A butler. Isn't that what fancy gentlemen's clubs have? Or maybe some kind of a security guard. Even our house had a housekeeper answer the door—at least, before. Before we fell from grace.

Before my world fell apart.

The man makes no move to speak, to invite me in or turn me away. Instead he stares at me with vague curiosity, with a trace of pity, the way one might watch an animal in the zoo. That might be how the whole world looks to these men, who have more money than God, more power than the president.

That might be how I looked at the world, before.

My throat feels tight, as if my body fights this move, even while my mind knows it's the only option. "I need to speak with Damon Scott."

Scott is the most notorious loan shark in the city. He deals with large sums of money, and nothing less will get me through this. We have been introduced, and he left polite society by the time I was old enough to attend events regularly. There were whispers, even then, about the young man with ambition. Back then he had ties to the underworld—and now he's its king.

One thick eyebrow rises. "What do you want with him?"

A sense of familiarity fills the space between us even though I know we haven't met. This man is a stranger, but he looks at me as if he wants to know me. He looks at me as if he already does. There's an intensity to his eyes when they sweep over my face, as firm and as telling as a touch.

"I need…" My heart thuds as I think about all the things I need—a rewind button. One person in the city who doesn't hate me by name alone. "I need a loan."

He gives me a slow perusal, from the nervous slide of my tongue along my lips to the high neckline of my clothes. I tried to dress professionally—a black cowl-necked sweater and pencil skirt. His strange amber gaze unbuttons my coat, pulls away the expensive cotton, tears off the fabric of my bra and panties. He sees right through me, and I shiver as a ripple of awareness runs over my skin.

I've met a million men in my life. Shaken hands. Smiled. I've never felt as seen through as I do right now. Never felt like someone has turned me inside out, every dark secret exposed to the harsh light. He sees my weaknesses, and from the cruel set of his mouth, he likes them.

His lids lower. "And what do you have for collateral?"

Nothing except my word. That wouldn't be worth anything if he knew my name. I swallow past the lump in my throat. "I don't know."

Nothing.

He takes a step forward, and suddenly I'm

crowded against the brick wall beside the door, his large body blocking out the warm light from inside. He feels like a furnace in front of me, the heat of him in sharp contrast to the cold brick at my back. "What's your name, girl?"

The word *girl* is a slap in the face. I force myself not to flinch, but it's hard. Everything about him overwhelms me—his size, his low voice. "I'll tell Mr. Scott my name."

In the shadowed space between us, his smile spreads, white and taunting. The pleasure that lights his strange yellow eyes is almost sensual, as if I caressed him. "You'll have to get past me."

My heart thuds. He likes that I'm challenging him, and God, that's even worse. What if I've already failed? I'm free-falling, tumbling, turning over without a single hope to anchor me. Where will I go if he turns me away? What will happen to my father?

"Let me go," I whisper, but my hope fades fast.

His eyes flash with warning. "Little Avery James, all grown up."

A small gasp resounds in the space between us. He already knows my name. That means he knows who my father is. He knows what he's done. Denials rush to my throat, pleas for understanding. The hard set of his eyes, the broad strength of his shoulders tells me I won't find any mercy here.

I square my shoulders. I'm desperate but not broken. "If you know my name, you know I have friends in high places. Connections. A history in this city. That has to be worth something. That's my collateral."

Those connections might not even take my call, but I have to try something. I don't know if it will be enough for a loan or even to get me through the door. Even so, a faint feeling of family pride rushes over my skin. Even if he turns me away, I'll hold my head high.

Golden eyes study me. Something about the way he said *little Avery James* felt familiar, but I've never seen this man. At least I don't think we've met. Something about the otherworldly glow of those eyes whispers to me, like a melody I've heard before.

On his driver's license it probably says something mundane, like brown. But that word can never encompass the way his eyes seem almost luminous, orbs of amber that hold the secrets of the universe. *Brown* can never describe the deep golden hue of them, the indelible opulence in his fierce gaze.

"Follow me," he says.

Relief courses through me, flooding numb limbs, waking me up enough that I wonder what I'm doing here. These aren't men, they're animals. They're predators, and I'm prey. Why would I willingly walk inside?

What other choice do I have?

I step over the veined marble threshold.

Want to read more? The Pawn is available on Amazon, iBooks, Barnes & Noble, and other book retailers!

Books by Skye Warren

Endgame Trilogy & more book in Tanglewood

The Pawn

The Knight

The Castle

The King

The Queen

Escort

Survival of the Richest

The Evolution of Man

The Bishop

Mating Theory

North Security Trilogy & more North brothers

Overture

Concerto

Sonata

Audition

Chicago Underground series

Rough

Hard

Fierce

Wild

Dirty

Secret

Sweet

Deep

Stripped series

Tough Love

Love the Way You Lie

Better When It Hurts

Even Better

Pretty When You Cry

Caught for Christmas

Hold You Against Me

To the Ends of the Earth

Standalone Dangerous Romance

Wanderlust

On the Way Home

Hear Me

For a complete listing of Skye Warren books, visit

www.skyewarren.com/books

About the Author

Skye Warren is the New York Times bestselling author of dangerous romance such as the Endgame trilogy. Her books have been featured in Jezebel, Buzzfeed, USA Today Happily Ever After, Glamour, and Elle Magazine. She makes her home in Texas with her loving family, sweet dogs, and evil cat.

Sign up for Skye's newsletter:
www.skyewarren.com/newsletter

Like Skye Warren on Facebook:
facebook.com/skyewarren

Join Skye Warren's Dark Room reader group:
skyewarren.com/darkroom

Follow Skye Warren on Instagram:
instagram.com/skyewarrenbooks

Visit Skye's website for her current booklist:
www.skyewarren.com

COPYRIGHT

This is a work of fiction. Any resemblance to actual persons, living or dead, business establishments, events or locales is entirely coincidental. All rights reserved. Except for use in a review, the reproduction or use of this work in any part is forbidden without the express written permission of the author.

Mating Theory © 2020 by Skye Warren
Print Edition

Cover design by Book Beautiful
Formatted by BB eBooks

Printed in Great Britain
by Amazon

71922334R00139